Death Spiral

Holly Hamilton

Ukiyoto Publishing

All global publishing rights are held by

Ukiyoto Publishing

Published in 2023

Content Copyright © Holly Hamilton

ISBN 9789360167776

All rights reserved.
No part of this publication may be reproduced, transmitted, or stored in a retrieval system, in any form by any means, electronic, mechanical, photocopying, recording or otherwise, without the prior permission of the publisher.

The moral rights of the author have been asserted.

This is a work of fiction. Names, characters, businesses, places, events, locales, and incidents are either the products of the author's imagination or used in a fictitious manner. Any resemblance to actual persons, living or dead, or actual events is purely coincidental.

This book is sold subject to the condition that it shall not by way of trade or otherwise, be lent, resold, hired out or otherwise circulated, without the publisher's prior consent, in any form of binding or cover other than that in which it is published.

www.ukiyoto.com

For Darla whose passion for figure skating inspired me to write this book.

Contents

How It Happened (Callum's POV)	1
Dreaming Again (Callum's POV)	4
Tell Me More (Callum's POV)	7
I Have No Idea (Callum's POV)	10
The Agreement (Elisia's POV)	14
The Visit (Elisia's POV)	17
Handsome (Callum's POV)	21
Mutual Attraction (Elisia's POV)	24
The Memory (Callum's POV)	27
Nothing Special About Me (Elisia's POV)	30
The Other Memory (Callum's POV)	34
The Coaching Job (Callum's POV)	37
Bruno (Elisia's POV)	41
Jealousy (Callum's POV)	45
Back on Ice (Elisia's POV)	48
Being Professional Sucks (Callum's POV)	53
Student and Teacher (Elisia's POV)	56
The Professional (Callum's POV)	59
More than Friends (Elisia's POV)	62
Let Go (Callum's POV)	66
The Fakers (Elisia's POV)	71
If You'll Let Me (Elisia's POV)	74
Callum's POV	78
On Thin Ice (Elisia's POV)	81
Death Spiral (Callum's POV)	86
Defeating Demons (Elisia's POV)	90
The Competition (Callum's POV)	93
About the Author	*97*

How It Happened (Callum's POV)

You'll *be a champion, Callum. You'll take home the Gold. All you and Ginger have to do is nail every move between now and nationals.*

My coach made it sound like winning was everything. But on the road to winning, I lost myself. I lost everything and everyone I cared about for a stupid medal. If I could take it all back, I would. Because losing Ginger's life is not worth ice skating.

"Callum, wake up? Are you still thinking about Ginger? You need to let that go. It has been over a year since she died. Ginger wouldn't want you moping over her death, she'd want you back out there winning medals."

That's my coach trying to make sense of it all. Ginger wasn't just my ice-skating partner; she was my life partner. It was my job to make her look her best on the ice and to make sure she was safe. I failed to do my job because showing off and fame got in the way. One knee wobble made my ego slip and Ginger's life end.

The day Ginger died, the ice was covered in blood, and her head injury was my fault. They tell me it could have happened to anyone. That pair skating is the most dangerous, and that dancing with blades means injury and possible fatality. They only tell you that, but when it becomes reality, it makes the world spin.

The color red brings out my inner turmoil. It's the color of betrayal and my ego getting in the way. I wanted to show off to the world. I tossed Ginger into the air and miscalculated when it was time to catch her. I didn't catch her on time, and she landed head-first on the ice. I touched her hand before she landed. She tried to land on her left skate. But her body wouldn't turn around, and her head shattered on the frozen ice below her skull.

The audience gasped, and the medics skated toward me. The cameras were rolling as the microphones found my lips. I had nothing to say. No comment to make. My system was shocked, and any dream of pair skating with Ginger in the Olympics failed.

We were always in perfect synchronization. We were the best of the best, but even the best failed. I became the biggest failure of them all. Ginger Yopp my dearest love, fell to her death and my heart broke alongside her head in that competition. They closed the rink early that day, and the rest of it was a blur.

I remember Ginger on life support with a heart monitor beeping faintly. It all stopped as her last breath gave way. I held her hand as the coma became death. As death became fear, and as fear became solitude. I became a lone wolf, without a mate. I no longer had meaning or joy. Only tears, beer, and countless days beside a headstone.

"Ginger Yopp, beloved daughter, and fiancé." That is what her headstone said. But she was so much more than that. She was the magic of the ice, and no one would ever replace her. I vowed to never skate again.

"I can't, Coach Ping. I can't skate anymore. Please stop coming here. I can't bring myself to lace up my skates and pretend nothing happened. I'm not ready."

"Will you at least come and sign a couple of autographs at the youth competition this weekend? It would mean the world to them to see a professional, such as yourself."

Coach Ping will say anything to get me to enter the arena building. I haven't set foot inside the building since Ginger died. I don't have the stomach for it.

"Don't you have some other ex-professional skater to annoy? Ask Adam Rippon to sign autographs for you," I ask.

"He's not available. Only you are available, and I am only asking you. You don't have to skate or set foot on the ice. You have my word."

Coach Ping surrenders it all, her hands give up and the ball is in my court. The ball is always in my court.

"Alright, I can sign a few autographs for the young skaters. But I am not performing or commenting. I don't want to be interviewed about anything. If you can keep microphones out of my face you have yourself a deal."

I hold out my hand to shake Coach Ping's hand. She firmly shakes it back.

"I will do the best I can to keep the journalists away. But sooner or later you will have to face what happened. I am not saying you need to be interviewed to face it, but someday Callum another woman might waltz into your life, and when she does you might want to tell her about Ginger and what she meant to you."

I know Coach Ping means well, but the chances of me falling in love again are slim to none. Ginger was my end game, and now she is gone. I am planning on being single for the rest of my life. Anyway, it's my business and no one else's. Coach Ping leaves as I prepare for the upcoming youth competition. I get on my laptop and look for a new outfit on Amazon. I could always use a new outfit to sign autographs in. If Ginger was here, she would convince me to join the civic arena and take the job. It's hard to accept a job when I know Ginger's ghost will haunt me somehow.

"I love you, Callum..." Ginger's voice haunts me.

"I'm sorry Ginger, it's time I returned to the place where you slipped out of my reach. Please forgive me." I will never be able to forgive myself, but maybe Ginger can lay to rest if I let her go.

Dreaming Again (Callum's POV)

"*Isn't it beautiful, Callum? An audience is chanting our names listen." The sound of 'Ginger and Callum" can be heard from around the stadium. It echoes like a thunderous applause.*

"They really like us. Let's get ready to skate." Ginger rests her head on mine and finds my hands. She prays for us like she does before every performance and practice we undertake together. I am not a religious man, but I believe in the power of prayer. Her prayers are guidance and praise from the higher power who gave us our ability to engage an audience.

The music begins as we find our skates on the ice. The fridged air means I haven't made a sweat yet. Ginger's hands clasp mine and our routine begins. We start with a pair sequence and are in perfect synchronization. The audience claps as we make our first lift. I lift her effortlessly as she floats through the air like a cloud.

We skate toward the middle and perform a death spiral. I hold her skate as she is lowered to the ground. My body becomes a pivot anchoring her from spinning out of control.

Our next move is the twist lift, where Ginger must twist three times in the air. We have struggled with this move-in practice, but I am confident we can nail it today. Ginger smiles at me as I lift her, and as she twists and falls back toward me, I miscalculated how far away she would land. I am not close enough as our hands touch. Ginger lands headfirst on the ice. The blood leaves her head, and the ringing in my ears is the sound of white noise. Fight, flight, and freeze have blurred into one. I pick Ginger's head up on my lap as the medics come. They take her away from me, and that's the last of it. It's the end of our skating career and future life together.

"Callum O'Leary is that you?" The memory of Ginger's death fades. The Civic Arena is still as chilly as I remember. The sound of skates scraping the ice makes me want to vomit.

"Hello, Coach Ping. I thought I had it in me to come back here. But I don't. I can't be here. The sound of skates makes me think of her."

"Let me show you something, Callum, before you decide to leave," Coach Ping says. I follow the coach as she takes me to the wall of medals.

"This is a memorial for Ginger. It tells her story and her victories. There are pictures of you two together. I just wanted you to know it's here. I've seen skaters place flowers in front of it before a competition. I think you should stay awhile and see what I mean. It might surprise you. At least stay for the first half of the competition. Sign a few autographs and leave. No interviews, I paid the journalists to leave you alone."

I sit down at the table in front of the medal display.

"You did? Well, now I can't leave then. Alright, I will stay for an hour if it would mean that much to you. But not a minute more."

A young blonde woman walks up to the glass window and places them under Ginger's picture. She mutters a quick prayer as she closes her eyes.

"Excuse me, did you know Ginger?" I ask, not sure if I have seen this woman before.

"No, I admired her though. My name is Elisia. I'm just a fan of Ginger's. I miss watching her perform. Her partner and she were amazing. Wait a minute, you look an awful lot like the man in the picture."

Elisia turns her head back and forth and compares my face to the competition photo.

"I miss Ginger. She was the best partner I ever had." Coach Ping smiles as I shake Elisia's hand.

"I just want you to know she meant an awful lot to me. And I am so sorry for your loss. Would you mind signing this napkin? I would love to have your autograph if that's okay."

Coach Ping hands me a pen and nudges me to sign the napkin.

Brochures pop out from the wall, and I grab one. I sign the brochure next to the old picture of Ginger and me from five years ago.

"Wow, thanks. I didn't even think about the brochures. Can I get a photo with you too?"

"Elisia, stop talking to this man and come here now. We have rehearsal today in the next rink over or did you forget?" A cranky young man snaps at her. Elisia's happiness wanes as she takes a quick selfie with me.

"Derek relax this is Callum O'Leary, he's the guy who used to compete with Ginger."

It's nice that she didn't call Ginger the dead woman like a rude person might have.

"It's nice to meet you, Callum. Thanks for taking a picture with Elisia. She can be a handful. We are practicing in the next arena over. Enjoy the competition." Derek's half-smile makes him as friendly as an unripe grapefruit.

"Thanks, and good luck with practice." Elisia waves at me, as a crowd of people point at me. A group of cameras and people sit in front of me, and the autographs begin. All I want to do is leave and forget about ice skating. The only nice person I met today was Elisia. I will never forget the way she prayed in front of Ginger's photo. It was like Ginger's spirit reached through the photo and prayed for me today.

Thanks, Ginger, for blessing me today with your prayerful presence, I could not have done it without you.

I sign the last autograph and leave after an hour. I will never again return to the Civic Arena; I have no reason to. It's comforting to know that Ginger's memory is honored by current skaters and it's enough for me to move on and never skate again.

Tell Me More (Callum's POV)

"Callum, wait don't leave. I was hoping you could tell me more about Ginger," Elisia yells as she runs after me in the parking lot. The snow is blowing and it's early January. She's in her performance outfit and is running after me, a has-been memory.

"Elisia, is it? I'll walk you back inside. I really don't want to talk about Ginger. You didn't do anything wrong by asking, I'm just not ready. To tell you the truth, I hardly had it in me to come here today."

Elisia puts her hand on my arm and lets me escort her back into the building. The reflection on the automatic door shows Elisia's smile.

"Thank you, Mr. O'Leary, it's been an honor meeting you," Elisia says as she lets go of me. Her movements and height remind me of Ginger. Her prayers before practice bring back the skating memories, and in front of a total stranger, I shed a single tear.

"Callum, it's time for us to go," Coach Ping says as she helps me leave the Civic Arena.

"I'll see you around, Elisia." *Elisia, what a strange delight you are among strangers.*

Coach Ping takes my car keys and offers to drive. I allow it because this is all too much. The memorial to Ginger. The woman whose very presence resembles the woman I have lost and will never see again.

"Thanks for driving me, coach. I must ask you, did that girl remind you of Ginger?"

"No, Callum. Ginger was a redhead and Elisia is a blonde. I think you are grieving and want to see Ginger in every woman you meet."

But Coach Ping is wrong. Elisia's mannerisms match my Ginger's, and it was enough to make me want to go back there and tell her all about Ginger.

"Coach, can we go back? I think I left my wallet inside." It's a small fib, but the coach doesn't question it and does a donut in the icy parking lot.

"When we get back, we will discuss your future. I have a proposition for you."

Another proposition to recruit me into the skating world. I miss my name being adored by fans in the stadium and the classical music I would perform too. But none of it feels real anymore, I am a ghost in the void without Ginger to show off on ice. She was the shining star that I held up and people admired. Now she is a memory on the wall, and it's about time I visit her graveside.

I get out of the car and run into the Civic Arena. Derek is yelling at Elisia, and her eyes are pink.

"I don't know why I waste my time with you. You are the worst partner in the history of figure skating. My coach said you would take me to the Olympics. You can't even land correctly when I lift you."

"I told you, Derek, I am doing the best I can. I just got out of the hospital six months ago. Let's see how well you can land while getting yelled at," Elisia says, as Derek lifts a backhand toward Elisia's face.

"That's a warning," Derek says. I take my hand and pull his away from Elisia's face.

"No, this is a warning. If I ever catch you threatening a woman in my presence ever again you prick, it will be the last thing you'll remember before you're put behind bars. Are we clear?" I ask as I twist his arm behind his shoulder.

"I yield, I yield. Jesus, man I was only joking," Derek says.

"If you're only joking then why are Elisia's eyes red? Seems to me she needs a new partner," I say standing between both of them.

"What was that? Everyone knows how you let Ginger fall to her death. You miscalculated and she had to pay the price. I've seen the YouTube video. No wonder you became a drunk lonely man who is too scared to skate again. At least I try."

Elisia stands up and her blonde hair covers her red eyes from me.

"He's right, Derek. I need a new partner. I think you should leave."

"What did you just say to me? You can't quit the competition is tomorrow," Derek scowls at both of us.

"Then I suggest you sign up for one of the singles events because the only person who wants to partner with you is your own reflection. It's over, Derek. I can't take the commentary anymore."

Elisia grabs my hand and leads me out of the Civic Arena. Derek continues to yell, as Coach Ping pulls the car around the corner.

"What in the world happened and what is she doing here," Coach Ping asks as Elisia buckles up her seat belt.

"She's coming to lunch with us, Coach," I reply. Elisia's eyes are still red, and I have a feeling she will cry while the competition is happening.

"Does she even want to come to lunch with us?" Coach Ping asks as she accelerates my car faster than I am comfortable with.

"Yes, that would be lovely. I needed to get away from Derek. I just broke up with him. I won't be competing with him tomorrow."

Coach stops at a red light and turns around to face Elisia.

"I'm sorry to hear that. Don't wait too long to tell your coach. They will need to take you out of the program, so they don't announce you."

Coach Ping pulls into *Panera*, and I get out and open Elisia's door. Her presence reminds me of Ginger, and it's hard not to feel a little sad on the inside. I follow Coach Ping inside and mentally prepare for the proposition of a lifetime.

I Have No Idea (Callum's POV)

Panera Bread smells like flour, butter, and soup. I haven't been since Ginger insisted, we spend time together. Back then it was forbidden to date a skating partner. I didn't care about the rules, I only cared about her, my red-haired queen.

Rules were meant to be tested and broken. Did Coach Ping and the Skating Club think I wouldn't develop feelings for the woman who I lifted toward the heavens? It was unnatural to keep us apart. Ginger was the only woman I ever cared about, and Elisia's mannerisms are uncanny and hard not to notice.

I fidget in my pocket for my wallet. I am keen to pay for everyone. I owe Coach Ping a bit of gratitude for keeping the journalists away and Elisia was kind to me and paid respects to Ginger.

"What would you like to eat?" I ask as I get my credit card out.

"A Sierra turkey. It's off-menu actually they don't technically make them anymore."

Her eyes are green, the same as Ginger's. Ginger had freckles and frizzy red hair. Elisia has no freckles, and her blonde hair is straight. Then why does Ginger's spirit live within the woman before me?

"Ginger used to eat that, too. Sorry, I know you were a fan of hers. She would have laughed that your sandwiches matched, I imagine. Excuse me, I'll take two Sierra Turkeys, and Coach what would you like to eat?" I ask as the Panera cashier taps her nails on the counter.

"I'll have a Caesar salad and I'd like mac and cheese without the cheese."

The cashier scratches her head at Coach's order.

"Did you say you want Mac and cheese without the cheese? So, you want noodles then?" Coach Ping nods.

"I can't help that I am lactose intolerant," Coach Ping says.

I hand my credit card to the impatient cashier. We find a table in front of the little fireplace. Its presence is warm and soothing.

"Thanks for lunch, Callum. You really didn't have to do that," Elisia says as I pull a chair out for her.

Coach Ping waits for our order to be called before giving me the details of our meeting. Our order is called through the loudspeaker, "Ginger, your order is ready." I pick up the trays and head back toward our seats.

"Ginger, huh? You even use her name for your restaurant alias," Elisia asks.

"Yeah, it's out of habit I suppose. I'll go get some silverware. Be right back." I dash to the line and grab some extra napkins and silverware.

"Here's your mac and cheese, Coach. And a Sierra turkey for you, Elisia."

"Thanks, I really appreciate your kindness, especially after Derek's outburst at the arena. I do apologize for that; his comments were uncalled for. I'd say he doesn't mean it, but he's been saying a lot of cruel things lately. I don't want to lie on his behalf, and I don't want to be his partner anymore. I guess I will be joining the singles events and representing myself. There's nothing wrong with that though, plenty of other skaters skate without a partner."

She takes small bites of her meal like a tiny bird. It's not fair to compare Elisia to Ginger, they are two different people. Their mannerisms may be similar, but one is dead and the other is in front of me breathing.

"So, tell me, Coach, what is the proposal you have for me today?"

"I'll cut right to it. The arena is looking for an assistant coach to work with me. They wanted me to ask you."

An assistant coach position? Not that I like my life right now. But after today it is clear that the Arena wants nothing to do with me. Maybe Derek was right that it is all my fault and that I am a coward.

"An assistant coaching job? I don't know, Coach Ping. That doesn't sound like a good idea," I reply.

"Everyone loved seeing you back in the arena and it's not competition. You'll be fine," Coach Ping says.

"I'm not interested. What if I make a fool of myself?"

"You won't make a fool of yourself. What do you think, Elisia? You'd be his student," Coach says while ignoring my clear distress at this proposition.

"I'd rather not say," Elisia says, trying to be diplomatic. At least she has enough sense to stay out of the issue. Coach Ping planned this right from the beginning. She knew I might be willing to sign autographs and then planned to ask me afterward, it's clever really.

"Very well, Callum, what are you choosing to do? I need you and so does the arena. Your days of sulking over Ginger are over. Students need you; I need you."

"I don't appreciate you pressuring me like this. You know what a screw-up I am."

"You aren't a screw-up, Callum. I was there when Ginger fell during the accident. As skaters we know the risks, it could have happened to anyone. It's not your fault and it doesn't define you," Elisia says, as she covers her mouth when I turn toward her.

Maybe she's right. I don't need to be labeled and judged for Ginger's death. But deep within I feel like a cold-blooded killer that the hounds forgot to devour.

"You really think I can do this? You hardly know me and you're that confident? Can you sit there and tell me I am not responsible for Ginger's death," I say as I rise out of my chair.

"Sit down, Callum. You are making a scene," Coach Ping says as she hands me her bag of chips.

"You aren't responsible for her death," Elisia says as she turns and whispers into Coach Ping's ear. The whole thing is making me uncomfortable as they chatter quietly while looking back and forth at me.

"What is going on over there?" I ask knowing I will regret it.

"How about a different job then, Callum?" Coach asks.

"Yeah, and what's that exactly?"

"How would you like to be my new partner," Elisia asks, as I sit there not knowing how to reply. I know that whatever I say next, will either make or break me.

Ginger, if you're up there please tell me what to do because I have no idea.

14

The Agreement (Elisia's POV)

"**H**ow would you like to be my new partner," I ask again. Callum's eyebrows raise and the lines on his forehead indent. He has no interest in trying again. Ginger was his first and only. I know the age gap between us is at least six years, maybe eight. But I know how talented he is, how passionate he could be on the ice. If only he would let himself feel that fire again. It's not his fault Ginger hit her head on the ice, and that she died. As skaters, we are taught the risks and know what might happen.

"I'm sorry I can't. Excuse me, I need to get going," Callum says. He gets up from his chair and stares at his garbage. He smiles at me half-heartedly and carries my tray over to the trash can.

"Callum, we rode here together. How are you getting out of here?" Coach Ping asks.

"It's called Uber. Mine will be here soon. I'll see you around, Elisia. Thanks again for asking me. I'm not the right person to skate with you and Coach, I am not ready to teach skating again. I am not ready for any of this. Please don't ask me again," Callum's teeth grind as his jaw makes a loud squeak sound.

"I'm sorry. I didn't mean to upset you. It was nice to meet you today. Thanks for the meal. If you'd ever want to watch me compete in the singles event, I would love to have you there. And I didn't know Ginger, but I can't imagine she would want you to give up your passion so easily."

Callum leaves and doesn't reply. I know I've hurt him, but he needed to hear it. He turns around as the Uber driver pulls up.

"You have no right to talk about Ginger like that. I think it best if we never see each other again. I'm sorry, I can't do this."

The trembling of his voice means he is alone. It whispers like a ghost in the valley of lost souls.

"I didn't mean to upset him, Coach Ping. I thought he would want to compete again. Ginger died a year ago and I know I've only just met him."

"Elisia, stop. It's not you. Today was his first day back in the arena since the accident. He's in shock. Give him some time, he'll come around. I pushed him too far, that's on me. For now, just avoid Derek and enter the singles events. I'll clear my schedule next week to train you. It's on the house."

Coach Ping throws her trash away. I follow behind her and head back to the car.

"Are you sure I didn't upset him?"

"Not a chance. He pulled me aside earlier and mentioned how you reminded him of Ginger. I didn't tell him this but I see it too. Your mannerisms and voice are very similar to hers. It's uncanny."

"Even if he does come around. It's probably better if I stand away. He made it clear that he doesn't want me around. And if I remind him of Ginger, that's like ripping a band-aid off the wound. Thanks for letting me know."

I buckle up my seat belt. Coach Ping puts on her sunglasses and clears her throat.

"Elisia, give Callum a chance. My hope for you is that you'll be able to skate with a partner again. And don't worry about Derek, I've already emailed your coach to tell them you won't be available to compete tomorrow. I've reserved the rink for Monday afternoon. Take tomorrow off and don't worry about missing the competition tomorrow. To tell you the truth Derek had it coming. How long were you partners?"

I wish I could tell Coach Ping the truth that skating with Derek was insufferable. But it wouldn't help me one bit. Our time together is done, and I have no intention of skating with someone so reckless ever again.

Callum always caught Ginger, except that one time. I've studied their pair skating videos enough times, to know he always counted every step she took. It was human error that killed Ginger, not Callum. When

Derek does lifts with me, I am fearful. I'd rather partner with someone more experienced, who counts every step their partner takes.

I know Callum will never go for someone like me. He's too hurt by skating and too angry at himself to enjoy it ever again. Getting close to Callum or even befriending him would only hurt him and bring those memories of Ginger back. I can't change who I am or how I act, and I don't want to dim my inner lights for Callum. If my inner fire is telling me anything, it's telling me to back off and let him come to me, when and if he's ready.

"I was partnered with Derek for about three years. Three years too long if you ask me. Thanks for taking me on for the singles competition. You didn't have to do that."

"Not a problem, dear. You have the potential to win medals and if I am lucky, win over a certain stubborn male skater back to the arena. "

"So, you are using me to get to, Callum? I knew there was a catch."

"That's why I am not charging you for our lessons. If he doesn't come back within six months, consider our time together terminated. Do we have a deal," Coach Ping asks as she stops at a red light and holds out her hand to shake mine.

"Before I shake your hand, what am I agreeing to exactly?"

"I want you to convince Callum to become your skating partner. Do whatever you have to to get him to return to the ice. Just don't fall in love with him, he's had enough drama in that area for a lifetime. Once you get him to come back, I will pay you for your help."

Without thinking and before the light turns green, I shake Coach Ping's hand. I don't know what I am getting myself into, but I only hope that Callum will let me become his friend.

The Visit (Elisia's POV)

Have you ever done something so stupid that you wanted to beat yourself up for it? That's how I feel right this very second. What was I thinking about agreeing to get Callum to come back to skating? He has made it very clear to me that he wants nothing to do with ice skating or Ginger. He was repulsed at himself for enjoying my company, for now, I know that I remind him of Ginger.

Could Ginger be the reason he returns to skating? If I could somehow remind him of what skating meant to them. It's a way for him to keep her legacy going. Her legacy is worshipped online, and everyone who follows skating knows about Ginger and Callum.

Coach Ping might have warned me to stay away from Callum. If I fell in love with him, it would be the end of everything. I've already ended it with Derek, who was my secret fling. I am not about to throw myself into someone else's thoughts. For I don't even want to be in my own thoughts.

My thoughts are a terrible poison before a competition. Maybe Derek shouting at me was cruel, but it was also motivational to keep me going. I have always been a little shaky on my left ankle, a result of a childhood injury. I've gone to physical therapy and have done all I can. Despite all the medicine in the world, I will never be an Olympian. It was my dream, but now I can have another dream. My new dream is to help Callum fall in love with skating again.

I suspect that for Callum every day is an endless nightmare, filled with memories of that day Ginger died. He replays it over and over and lets it poison him. The thing about poison is that with the right medicine and a little patience, it can be removed. He needs healing and I am going to be the one to heal him.

I sit on my apartment couch, with a frozen meal. I don't have time for cooking which is unfortunate. Athletes are supposed to have diets like gods. My diet is anything but that. It is filled with canned food, frozen that, and premade meals. I didn't have time to learn how to cook in college, that was for the other woman who wanted to be a homemaker. For me, being a homemaker wasn't the dream, only skating.

Floating on ice and gliding through the rink was where my feet were meant to be. The scraping of ice as it makes snow, the drip of water on my blades. The sweat of perfection spun with my stance. My passion follows me with each extra minute of practice. I know what determination is, and that this world of being perfect is lonely. That's the last place, Callum should be. He doesn't deserve to be alone, cast aside as the former victor. He could still be glorious and could still win if only he saw what I did.

I text Coach Ping to find out where Callum lives.

Me: Hi, Coach. Thanks for the ride home.

Ping: No problem. Is there something I can help you with?

Me: What's Callum's address?

Ping: 533 South Parrot Street.

Me: Thanks. I am going to pay him a visit.

Ping: Why? This late. Good luck.

Me: I will let you know later. Bye.

I type in Callum's address on my phone. I put two frozen meals in a plastic bag. I don't cook, but maybe he is hungry. The evening streets are empty and a train echoes in the background faintly.

I pull into an apartment complex. I didn't expect Callum to live alone in an apartment complex like me, I imagined him having a mansion. This only proves how much I know about the guy.

Me: Coach which apartment is his?

Ping: 32 C. You're wasting your time. I told you to give him space.

Me: I'll remember that.

His flat is on the third floor, and I climb the stairs all the way. I knock on his door with the bag of frozen dinners at my side. This was a bad idea, but it is too late he has opened the door.

"Elisia, what are you doing here it's so late?" I hand Callum the frozen dinners and turn around to leave.

"I see there are two dinners here. Did you want to come in," Callum asks as he opens the door further for me.

"Yeah, sure. I wanted to see how you were doing. And I wanted to apologize," I say as I walk into his apartment.

"What are you apologizing for?"

"Well, I obviously offended you. And I am sorry if I remind you of her. If my mannerisms or voice remind you of Ginger. Then tell me, so that when I am around you, I can change myself, so you don't get sad."

Callum leads me to his couch. He doesn't reply right away. And perhaps I wouldn't reply quickly either. This is an awkward situation.

"It's not you, Elisia. It's that I am not ready to be around the rink again. And I am sorry for being rude. I can see what you are trying to do, and we can be friends. Would you like me to heat these up for us?"

His smile stretches across his face and a few wrinkles appear on his forehead. He isn't old. But he is old enough for the stress to age him. The grey hairs are poking from the sides of his head where sideburns might be. He's handsome and I can see why Ginger fell for him. That thought makes my insides jump. No matter what Coach Ping says about Callum, he is someone who needs a friend.

"That would be great. I am starving. I wanted to ask you a quick question since I am here."

He opens the frozen meal packages and heats them up in his small kitchen. He turns the microwave on and gets the plates out.

"Sure, go ahead."

"Can you take me to meet Ginger, at her grave? I would love to pay my respects in person and not by an old memorial at the rink."

He hands me my plate of food. His smile turns into red eyes. I know I've touched his soul with my words. His vulnerability around me will make it hard to stay away. What if Coach Ping's warning was actually an encouragement to get Callum back into the rink?

"That would be lovely. And I don't want you to hide who you are around me, just because you remind me of Ginger. If Ginger were here, she'd tell you to be yourself."

I walk over to Callum and hug him. He's startled by my actions. But he needs human contact. The last person he ever touched was Ginger.

"I think she'd tell you to be yourself too and do the things that make you happy," I reply.

If Callum and I did fall for each other, I know deep down it would mean I am only a replacement for Ginger. I'm in no place to fall for anyone, but for some reason right now, I want to save Callum from himself and help him let go.

"What makes you happy, Elisia?"

"Playing board games," I reply as I see the mountains of games on his shelf.

"Let's play checkers," Callum smiles. That smile is going to be the reason I will disregard Coach's warning.

She did tell me to use whatever means necessary to help him return to the arena. That damn smile will get the best of me, and I might be okay with that. We play board games for hours as our frozen meals get cold. It's the first time that Callum has let someone else into his life, and I am not about to put that fire out.

"Can you take me to see Ginger's grave site? I can bring flowers and everything," I say as Callum wins the game of checkers. Our hands touch briefly as we collect the pieces of the game. I blush and look away. Nothing anyone can say will stop me from falling fast for Callum O'Leary. With a smile like that, I may have fallen just a little bit.

Handsome (Callum's POV)

"Can you take me to see Ginger's gravesite," Elisia asks as her blonde hair bobs up and down. It's not that I don't want to take Elisia, it's really quite sweet that she's even offered to join me and plant flowers beside her resting place. My bones sing a different song, one that could bring me life, and therapy, and help me heal. But I am afraid of healing, too stubborn to get on that train. To heal would mean I need to let go of Ginger and face the fact that she died. I am not ready to jump trains and have the rails sway beneath my feet, not if I have a say in the matter.

"Sure, we can visit Ginger's gravesite. I have been wanting to visit. But I am not sure I am ready to bring someone with me yet. The truth is, I don't know what is good for me anymore. I'm warning you now that a friendship with me could bring you unhappiness. That's all I know anymore."

"It's okay to be in a dark place, Callum. My mother passed away when I was twelve and I thought the world would end. I thought I wouldn't know how to move on, and I will always miss her. But I know whenever I skate, she is there looking down at me. So, I skate for her, I skate for my mom. Do you think you'll skate for Ginger someday? Maybe not now, but maybe years from now. Do you ever see yourself returning to the ice to celebrate her memory?"

The light grows dim, and the frozen meals Elisia brought have gone bad. Our checker's game lasted for three hours, and I am unaccustomed to having guests over.

"I don't know how to answer that question. I suppose maybe someday, I could skate to remember her. But not anytime soon. I'm not ready to put my blades on ice."

Elisia walks into my kitchen and throws our frozen meals away.

"I'm ordering us a pizza. I'll pay for it. What type of pizza do you want?"

Her eyes squint when she smiles. Her blonde hair falls on her shoulders. She's clearly younger than I am. I'm thirty. I am too old to compete in the Olympics anymore and too old for someone as young as Elisia.

"Pepperoni would be great. Elisia, how old are you? If you don't mind me asking."

"I'm twenty-one, almost twenty-two, why," Elisia asks as she pulls out her debit card.

"You seem mature for your age. I'm just feeling old. Well older than you anyway. I don't know if you noticed but my hair is a little grey on the sides. I miss being younger."

"You don't look old Callum. You're rather..." She pauses and looks up as if she is accessing the right words to use.

"Rather past my prime in the skating world, I know."

"No, you aren't, Callum. You aren't past your prime. Have you ever heard of Walter Jakobsson the Finnish skater? He won an Olympic gold medal at the age of thirty-eight. He was a pair skater."

"Who made you a Historian," I ask.

"My parents when they homeschooled me. I was fascinated by ice skating history, and they had me spend my senior year writing reports about famous skaters. My favorite was Michelle Kwan."

"I'm still older than you by quite a bit. I know you need a partner. I'm sorry Elisia, I can't be that for you. We've only just met."

Elisia turns and twists her body like a little kid fighting to stand still.

"I know we've just met. But the world isn't done with you yet. Let's go to Ginger's grave and you can see for yourself if you are ready to go back or not. But you aren't old. You are eight years younger than Walter Jakobsson, just a thought."

I smile at her, as her phone beeps. She checks it as her blue eyes scan the screen.

"The pizza is on its way, Callum. Then I will be leaving. I am sorry it's so late," Elisia says as she apologizes. It's hard to believe that someone I just met could have such an impression on me.

"You don't have to leave, it's almost midnight. We can eat the pizza and you could crash on the guest bed if you'd like. I have a few of Ginger's old clothes here. Maybe it's too weird for me to offer that. Don't feel like you have to stay."

Elisia smiles and sits down on the couch and makes herself at home. She sets up the checker's board again and signals to me that she wants a rematch.

"Thanks for the offer. I'd like to stay and see if I can beat you this time."

"We can play if you answer this one question," I reply.

She pauses as she finishes putting the final red piece on the board.

"Yeah, and what's that?"

"What were you going to say about me earlier? You never finished your sentence."

"Oh, that? I was saying that you aren't old you're rather...handsome."

The word *handsome* hasn't been used around me since Ginger died. She was the last girl I ever kissed, and the last girl I have ever been with.

"Thanks. You don't have to flatter me. I know you and Derek were engaged. I'm sorry you had to end that. It seems we are both emotionally, clouded."

"I'm not confused by anything, Callum. Yes, Derek and I were together. We broke up a while ago, we tried to keep skating together, but it was all a joke. You need to let yourself move on, Callum. We both need to move on," Elisia says as she sits a little closer to me.

"And how do you propose to move on exactly," I ask. Without rhyme or reason, Elisia puts her lips on mine. Her gentle lips startle me. She isn't Ginger, she doesn't smell or taste like her. I'm in love with a dead woman, and it's unfortunate because I would love to kiss Elisia back and actually mean it.

Mutual Attraction (Elisia's POV)

My lips are against Callum's and his lips tremble beneath mine. I stop the kiss he isn't ready for this; I pull away and he doesn't go in for more.

"I'm sorry, Callum. I shouldn't have done that. But I wanted to for some reason. We hardly know each other and yet I feel like I know you somehow. Well, anyway I'll be on my way. You enjoy the pizza and I'll see myself out."

Embarrassment consumes me. I've never kissed a guy first. I've always let the man initiate that. I'm sure I've done something wrong. The last woman he kissed was Ginger, and I've stolen that moment from him forever. It wasn't intentional, I never meant for this to happen. I never meant for my emotions to cloud my judgment.

I stand up and grab my purse. Callum stands up as well and grabs my hand. I'm not sure why he's grabbed my hands. Is it to affirm his anger and disgust of me?

"Listen, we both are just getting used to the other person. There's no reason to pretend we didn't kiss. We did. Maybe we can put a bookmark on this, and maybe when we are both ready and know each other more we can try again later. I don't want you to go because of one kiss. I offered to have you stay the night and I intend to let you do that. The guest bedroom is the first on the right. And please don't be embarrassed. I haven't kissed anyone since Ginger died, but that doesn't mean I won't move on eventually. It's just hard to let her go, we were supposed to be married and with kids by now. But my life spiraled beneath me. And now I don't know who I am. But we can still be friends, I am willing to be if you are."

His smile is contagious like everything else about him. His teeth are perfectly straight and white. Mine are crooked despite years of braces. His confidence makes my heart skip a beat and for some reason, I've already fallen a little bit more with each dialogue that passes between us.

"You have nice teeth, Callum. I just had to let you know. And I am sorry your life is spiraling that must have been terrifying for you. It sounds lonely. It's like the death spiral moves in pair skating, you are unevenly balanced and are spinning solo on the ice without a partner to hold hands with. If you let someone into your life maybe your world could be in balance once again and you could be an anchor in the middle of the ice holding someone else's hand as you skate."

Callum smiles at me again and his shiny teeth continue to blaze like a dim fire. Maybe he could be my anchor showing me off to cheering crowds as we pivot on the ice. That would take a lot of convincing on my part. He doesn't know me well enough yet to know I don't mean him any harm.

"Thanks, Elisia. Maybe you are right. It's a nice thought anyway. You know what I think I will take you to meet Ginger tomorrow."

"Oh, I would love that very much. Maybe we can buy some flowers for me to place at the gravesite. What was her favorite kind? What was her favorite meal? We could have a picnic in her honor or something."

Callum walks me to the bedroom and opens the closet. He shows me where Ginger's old clothes are.

"Yes, we could do that. It might be good to help me move on. Thanks for your help with everything. Please don't worry about the kiss, maybe one day when we kiss it will mean something. And I promise if that day ever comes, I won't hold back. I have a good feeling about you. So please continue to be my friend in the meantime."

He's so straightforward and kind. Unlike Derek, the world was a landmine full of bombs and eggshells. I never knew if my hand gestures or tone of voice would offend him and that made leaving him even more terrifying. Men like Derek have a quest for vengeance, and I know one day his wrath will be waiting out there for me. I only hope I will be able to avoid him before it gets to that.

"I'd love to be your friend. And thanks again for having me over. So what clothes am I allowed to wear?"

"Anything but her ice-skating uniforms. Those have memories attached to them."

The beautiful dresses are hung up in large plastic bags to protect them. Her medals and photos are all over the guest bedroom like one Ginger shrine.

"I'm intimidated by her success if I am honest. I was injured in my ankle when I was a kid, and I will never be fast or perfect at skating. I can pretend all I want, but these photos show a true champion."

Callum smiles again and turns the light off.

"Just keep practicing. You'll get there. As long as you enjoy it, I am sure you will do fine."

As he leaves the room, I grab his hand one more time. He stops and turns to look at me.

"You too, Callum. As long as you are interested in healing, I am sure you will be able to skate again for yourself one day," I reply.

"Can I kiss you one more time before I head to bed," Callum asks.

I put my lips on his and know that he is still guarding his heart. He closes his eyes, and a mutual attraction grows between us both. Coach Ping's warning shouts at me in the back of my head, but I disregard that inner voice and close my eyes in return. When he ends the kiss, I don't go in for more, I just hug him and turn out the remaining light.

The Memory (Callum's POV)

Two years earlier...

"Ginger, do you think you'll want kids?" I ask as Ginger puts her red hair behind her ear. We've only been engaged for a month but have been together for what feels like a lifetime. We have our whole future ahead of us and nothing will stand in our way.

"Yes, I suppose I do, Callum. It's in the cards for us. I hope they have red hair like mine. It would be an awful shame if they had your brown hair. Everyone has brown hair, but red hair means I have elf blood in my ancestry."

"Elf blood, hmmm? I don't think that's true," I say as I hand Ginger a mug of black coffee.

"My dad used to tell us stories about the red-haired elves who fought battles. I know it's not true, but it's a cool idea." Ginger sips her afternoon coffee, and the lights fade.

"How many kids would you like to have?"

"Three or four. How about you?"

"Three's a good number. I can't wait to start a family with you. When the wedding is done, we can become skating coaches and teach our children the ways of the ice."

"We don't have to wait until we are married to have kids," Ginger says as she goes into the kitchen and pulls out the fresh strawberries. She begins chopping them and heats up some waffles as well.

"What do you mean? Did you want to get married sooner?" I take the frozen waffles from Ginger and place them in the toaster oven. Ginger grabs my hand and places it on her stomach.

"I was going to wait to tell you, but now seems like a good time. I'm pregnant, Callum."

My eyes get big, and the excitement of fatherhood fills my mind. I don't care if it's a boy or a girl. They are my precious child, mine and Ginger's. I kiss her belly and place my head against it.

"Hello little one, this is Daddy. I am so excited to meet you soon."

Present-day:

"Callum, it's morning are we still going to go to the grave? You were tossing and turning a lot in your sleep is everything alright?"

The more I think about her question, the more I wonder if it's a trick question.

"I had a nightmare. I have them a lot." Elisia hands me my coffee and the memories of Ginger surface.

"I'm not ready to face, Ginger again. It's my fault she is gone. My fault my future is different."

Elisia grabs my hand and goes into the fridge and pulls out the frozen waffles and some strawberries.

It's like I am on repeat. I don't know if I am dreaming or asleep. I've been on autopilot since Ginger died on the ice. Elisia's mannerisms and choice of breakfast confuse me more and more.

"You don't have to face her. I just want to place roses at her graveyard. I can even go by myself if it would be easier. I made us a picnic lunch; well, they are only peanut butter sandwiches. To tell you the truth I am not much of a cook."

I am glad Elisia can't cook. It's how they are different. Ginger cooked all kinds of exotic dishes from all around the globe. It's how I know I am not dreaming.

"Ginger loved to cook. If I am honest, I don't know how to do anything anymore. I am all backward. I'm not ready to let her go, Elisia. Please, make me let her go."

"What was your dream about Callum? Did you dream about her?"

I know Elisia wants to pay her respects to her idol. But it's too much.

"It was about the day after we got engaged. Ginger and I were planning our futures together and things got emotional quickly. We talked about how many kids we wanted. Can you keep a secret even one that Coach Ping doesn't know about? If you say yes, I will be happy to take you to meet Ginger."

The toaster oven timer goes off and Elisia rushes over and takes the waffles out. I put the strawberries on top.

"Yes, I can. I won't tell anyone your secrets. I won't go breaking your confidence. Did I do something to offend you," Elisia asks as she hands me a plate.

"No, you didn't do anything. I have the same nightmare. It's not a nightmare, but it triggers my sadness when I wake up. So, anyway Ginger and I got to discuss our future together and she told me she was pregnant. She was going to have a little girl. Coach Ping never found out that I was going to become a father. And a few weeks later, Ginger passed away. I paid the doctors not to say anything about the pregnancy. Coach Ping would have suggested Ginger not compete in that competition. But she wanted to skate and told me she could handle it. She wasn't lying, she could handle it. But I was the fool who couldn't handle it. I had so many thoughts going on inside my head when I knew I wouldn't be there to catch her. Now I am loveless and childless. I think it best if you go to the grave by yourself today. I'm sorry Elisia, I am just not ready."

Elisia sits beside me and quietly takes a bite out of her waffles.

"Thanks for telling me. I won't tell Coach Ping. I'll leave flowers and a card and tell her you say hello. I'll let you know if she replies to me. Thanks for letting me stay over. And Callum, when you are ready to give us a chance, I'll be waiting. But until then, I can't wait to beat you at our next game of checkers."

Elisia places her dishes in the sink and kisses me on the cheek. A beautiful blonde woman is waiting for me, but I am not ready. No matter what I do, no matter how hard I cling to the past, if I don't let it go, I might miss out on a chance of newfound happiness and Ginger would want me to be happy. Then why do I not want happiness for myself?

Nothing Special About Me (Elisia's POV)

When the universe tells you to listen to the voices in front of you. You do it without question. Without rhyme or reason. It's the only thing keeping me going, the only reason I am able to continue as a figure skater.

I've won awards but not like Ginger. She was admired for always getting gold in the single events and revered for her pair skating.

Callum is a legend, and he doesn't know what he means to skaters. His very presence is the reason skaters fix their posture and sharpen their blades again. So, they too can be just as glorious as he is. If I could bring Callum back to the ice, I know he would be amazing.

I turn around and head back up the apartment stairs. His front door is still unlocked, I open the door a crack. Callum is crying on the couch holding a picture of Ginger. He whispers to Ginger's picture, and I overhear him.

"I'm sorry, I failed you, Ginger. I wish I could have caught you. I wish I could have had the chance for happiness. This is all my fault. We'd be a family if you were still here. I've met someone. She is different from the other girls; she wants to visit your grave. I think she is on her way; she means well. Don't hate me, darling, if I move on from us. But I need to heal. I don't know how to be myself anymore." He places his hands over his eyes and cries silently to himself.

"Callum, I'm back. You don't need to be alone anymore. It's okay to come out of the darkness and have friends. Ginger wherever you are, I want you to know I mean him well."

I take Callum's hand and have him rise to his feet. When he rises his height is taller than mine. I stand on my tiptoes and press my lips on Callum's, his tears are half dry on his face. But I don't mind, I wipe them away and wrap my hands around his neck when I do. He kisses me back, and it's then I know we both want this. Whatever this is starting between us, we both want to move forward but don't know how.

In skating and in dancing, the male takes the lead. It's his job to give the woman signals with his movements. These signals tell the woman what move is next so she can prepare herself. Today, Callum wasn't strong enough to tell me what to do or where to go. So I took the lead, and I am not used to doing so.

Callum pushes my body back on the couch, and I lie back as his gentle kisses become more. I don't push him for more and he doesn't push me. I don't think Coach Ping wanted me to get intimate with Callum, but I can't help it. I am involved now, and I'm attracted to him. He is handsome, but our age difference makes me feel like a fool. I've never dated anyone more than two years older than me, and he is at least eight or nine years older. But right now I don't care, I want him to choose me. I want to be the woman who saves him from himself.

Startlingly enough, I have let myself go so easily around a man I hardly even know. I've never let a man kiss me this much after a few interactions, but there was an immediate spark between us. Well, maybe more from me than him.

Callum's kiss deepens and his pecks turn into a French kiss as he puts his tongue in my mouth. I hum a little when he does and close my eyes as he kisses me. He gets off quickly and stops himself.

"I'm sorry, Elisia. I didn't mean to get so caught up in the moment. I promise it won't happen again. I need time to think all of this over. I am still confused about all of this," he says as he points to the space between us.

"I understand, Callum. For what it's worth. I enjoyed it. So don't hold back next time, if you ever want to do that again."

My heart pounds in my chest. It flutters beside my rib cage. Why do I care so deeply for the man who lost Ginger? I will never be Ginger enough for him. I'm not even a redhead, I am a blonde. But I want him to feel cared for, even by me the new woman in his life. My problem is I have always cared too much, too deeply, and too fast. It's my biggest character flaw and it will surely blow up in my face.

"Elisia, I appreciate what you are trying to do here. But I don't know if I am ready for this. Please don't push me, I don't know what I feel for you. I hardly know you."

My heart hardens and tightens around my chest. The big squeeze my muscles create by my heart forces a tear to shed.

"I know you don't know and neither do I. I just wanted to help you move on. I wanted to help you let go. I want to be there for you, but if you don't want me around...I understand. I'm sorry I'm not a redhead. I'm sorry I'm not her. I wish I was her, so you could be happy. I'm sorry I am not what you need. I was just trying to help you."

My words surprise him, they surprise me. Is it normal to feel like this for a stranger? Why do I care so much about this mopey jerk? He was a skating legend and I want to skate with him. But it's more than that, I know if more time passed, I would fall for him. He's the sort of man that I could fall for. And that is terrifying. I will never be Ginger, and he needs me to be. But why can't a hurt man, love someone else?

"Wait, *Ginger*, don't go." His words strike me like a thousand bullets. I've heard all I need to. He was using me to remember Ginger, and I can't skate with someone who will never see me for me.

"My name is Elisia Algora. Don't bother calling me, I think we know how this will turn out. I'm sorry I can't be the person you need me to be. I wish you luck, Callum. I really do. But I can't pretend to be someone who is dead. Even if your kisses made me happy for a moment, they aren't worth the heartache of not being Ginger enough for you. I thought this could turn into something amazing. But I was wrong, and I was foolish enough to start falling for you. What an idiot."

Callum's face turns red beside his cheeks. He wasn't supposed to hear the truth that I could fall for him. But what does it matter now? It doesn't matter at all, because the only woman he will ever love is Ginger.

"You're falling...for...me? Why? There's nothing special about me. You hardly know me."

"I don't know, Callum. But you're right about one thing, there is nothing special about you. You are just like all the other men who treat me like shit. I wanted to skate with you and help you be happy. But you don't want to be happy, you are living the same day over and over again in your head. I am not Ginger, and this facade needs to end. No matter what I feel for you or what I want to feel for you. This heartache isn't worth it."

I open the door and the rain is falling hard. I walk out into the rain and listen to it drop against the cars. The rain tells his story, he is in pain and only the sun will end his storm. I cry in the rain because somewhere in my bones, I have fallen for Callum O'Leary.

Callum follows me to my car, but I drive away afraid of the empty words he will say if I roll the window down to listen.

The Other Memory (Callum's POV)

Two years earlier:

"Callum, I'm pregnant. What do we do? We can't tell, Coach Ping. We have a big competition around the corner. We've been practicing for years; I can't let my pregnancy ruin that."

I know Ginger will want to compete, but Coach Ping and the arena have rules in place against women competing while pregnant.

"How far along are you?"

"The beginning of the second trimester. My bump is starting to show. I can't hide this in a costume."

She shows me her bump. I can hardly notice it.

"If we get new costumes no one will notice. Let's get new costumes."

"Good idea, Callum. I'll see who's available to make a new costume," Ginger says.

Present-day:

"Oh Ginger, what should I do? I can't hurt Elisia's feelings. She felt something in every single one of our kisses. I did too. But I didn't want to, Ginger. Am I betraying you if I fall for someone else? She's alive and wants me to be happy. What can I do to make it up to her, Ginger?"

I find myself talking at Ginger's photos a lot lately. I only hope she answers. To hear her voice again, I listen to all her voicemails and phone videos. When these videos or voicemails disappear, I will never remember what her voice sounds like. They are my deepest treasure. They are all I have left.

I scan through the voicemails I've saved and find one that she sent me three years ago on Valentine's Day. We weren't together at the time; I was off at a competition for the single men's events.

"Callum, I am so sorry we can't be together this year for Valentine's Day. Whenever you get this, I want you to know I love you. No matter where life takes us, sweetheart, just remember I will always love you no matter what. I want you to be happy. Do what you think is best. I am proud of you and happy Valentine's Day."

I play the message three more times. Even beyond the grave, she speaks to me like a mighty voice of echoes in an endless cavern. I do have some feelings for Elisia, but not as strong as I suspect her feelings are for me. We hardly know each other, but she said she's fallen for me. How is that possible? I've done nothing to deserve such high praise from a woman like her. I don't know if she notices or not, but our age difference is noticeable to me. She is eight or nine years younger than me; I will never be able to keep up with her. She is of the next generation and my youth is leaving me. I might have one more competitive season in me yet, but that's it.

We will never compete at the Olympics, and we will never be famous skaters together. My time with Ginger was the peak of my years. I call Coach Ping and act quickly on Elisia's behalf.

"Hello, what is it, Callum," Coach Ping asks sounding distracted.

"I've decided to take you up on your offer. I'd like to coach Elisia for the women's singles event. When can we start?"

"Excellent. Let's start in two days and Callum, I suggest you get your blades sharpened in the meantime. I am sure they are dull as hell by now. And don't tell anybody that you've agreed to this, not even Elisia. She is mad at you and won't tell me why?"

Coach Ping has a magical gift of sniffing out emotion. But not even her powers will work on me, for I am wiser now than I was years ago. Coach Ping doesn't need to know about Elisia and me, for there is nothing to tell. All we did was kiss, and I want to get to know her a little more before our lips meet again. If I push us into a corner too quickly, I fear I will lose Elisia the same way I lost Ginger...with my heart broken on the ice.

"She is mad because I turned down the coaching position. But I have reconsidered your offer. Anything else I should know."

"Yes, Callum you must promise me, you won't fall for Elisia. The last time you trained a woman you fell for her. And she is dead now. I am not saying this to be heartless, but I don't want you to get hurt. Don't let Elisia get into your head. You are her coach, first and only. I know you think she's beautiful, you kept comparing her to Ginger."

"I know she's not Ginger, Coach Ping. No one is. And don't worry about me liking Elisia, I am too old for her anyway."

"Yes, you are. You are an old man compared to the girl. She's recovering from a terrible breakup with her fiancé, Derek anyway. It's a shame really, they were predicted to go to the Olympics together and represent the United States. But that will never happen now that she refuses to skate with him."

Coach Ping never misses a beat. She was always on top of the latest gossip, which is why I am shocked that she never learned about Ginger's pregnancy. If she knew my lips have touched Elisia's, I would be out of a job and I am in no place to turn down another job just because depression has consumed my soul since Ginger died.

"Maybe we can find her a new partner. Maybe we could hold auditions for her. I know a few single-male skaters looking to transition over to pair skating."

Coach Ping breathes heavily into the phone. It hurts my ears.

"Yes, that's a wonderful idea. We will make flyers and advertise for her all-over social media. And with your own popularity as a legendary skater for our backing, we will get lots of men to skate with Elisia. Good idea, Callum."

I wish I never mentioned having an audition, a part of me is exhausted just thinking about it. But I had to do it for Elisia. She poured her heart out to me the other night, and I had to do something nice in return for her. Even if I can't skate with her, I can still coach her and help her train with a new partner. I hang up the phone and beg the skating gods to let Elisia forgive me and allow me to coach her.

The Coaching Job (Callum's POV)

Tryouts are stupid. I don't want to suffer through a bunch of cocky skaters for hours on end. Coach Ping has already set up a tryout page on the arena website and social media. Already twenty men have signed up in hopes of lifting Elisia into the air. I am not sure why this whole thing bothers me so much when it was my stupid idea. Most of my ideas are stupid.

It's early in the morning and my phone rings. The ringtone is loud, and I don't want to talk to anyone. The arena has already emailed me my coaching contract to fill out. They don't waste their time when it comes to hiring a new coach. Elisia is calling my phone, it's still too early for me to want to talk to anyone. I'd better pick it up though.

"Good morning, Elisia. How are you?"

"Don't play coy with me. I saw the advertisement on social media. Are you guys insane? Coach Ping wants me to get a new partner without talking to me about it and now I see your name in print as my new coach. When was this decided? You can't seriously want to be my coach after the other day. Are you trying to mess with me?"

"Woah, hold on a second. I thought you would be pleased that I was trying to make it up to you. I wasn't trying to hurt your feelings the other night, alright? You kissed me remember? I'm still confused about this whole thing too, I wasn't saying no to us trying it out, but as your coach I have to be professional now."

"Yeah, Callum. Because suddenly you are so professional. Up until a few days ago, you wanted nothing to do with the ice and now you are suddenly so willing to train me and some random male skater. What's your angle? What do you get out of it?"

She has a point. I wasn't trying to be a loser. I miss Ginger, but at the same time, I am drawn to Elisia. I guess I just want to make sure she's alright.

"I guess, I took the coaching job to get to know you better. But if you think I am messing with you, then I will just quit. You were so passionate about the ice, and I wanted to feel the same way about it that you did. I thought if I took the job, watching you train might make me not be so scared anymore. I just wanted to make sure you were all right. And I was hoping we could start over with a clean slate, so to speak. Can we start over and try being friends again? I won't deny I enjoyed the other night, but can we just focus on what's right in front of us now? Aren't I too old for you anyway?"

I hear a knock at the door. It's gentle and faint, as I open the door, I find a cold Elisia snuggled up to her phone. How long has she been there?

"Can I come in? It's freezing out here." Her cheeks are red, and the fall rain has been falling for a few hours now.

"Yes, please do. I'll go run you a hot bath. Don't freeze to death." I put a blanket around her shoulders and watch her shivering body in the mirror. Everything about her is tender and perfect. She is small and petite and would be easy to lift. Her blonde hair is soaked as well as her clothes. I pull her in for a hug, and she starts crying, her lips quiver and her trembling makes her squeak out a sigh.

"Thanks for letting me in. The truth is I don't know what I am doing back over at your place. I'm not mad at you, Callum. It's just hard to see someone so talented be in so much pain. I know you want a professional relationship, and we can try to do that. I will try. And maybe we can even become friends, but I do like you a little. So give me the benefit of the doubt. And who knows maybe this tryout will help me move on too."

The thought of her moving on from our little fling makes me a bit jealous. I try not to show it, but I can't help it.

"Thanks. That means a lot. I'll go start your bath and then make a pot of coffee. It's really early so if you want to take a nap, feel free to use the guest room. You know where it is, help yourself. And feel free to use any of Ginger's old things."

I don't head to the bath straight away. I stare at us in the mirror, we could be great together on the ice. She would be easy to lift, and we could be in perfect synchronization. But it's just not meant to be. I can't be with someone who is so much younger than me. An almost decade is a lot of difference. I turn around and she's still next to me, she rests her head on my shoulder. I lift up her head and she closes her eyes, inviting me back into where we left off the other night.

My hand finds the side of her cheek and she nestles it with her face when I do. She isn't trying to hide her affection toward me, she is straightforward with what she wants. And I am confused by it all. The woman I love is dead, and moving on is like performing for an audience. It starts out slowly and is nerve-wracking. Sure, we've kissed before, but the anticipation of our kiss is the same as the first lift. Will I be good at it, or will I cause us to fall into oblivion?

"Can you kiss me one more time, Callum? Before the world makes us have a professional relationship. If it's too much to ask, I understand."

No one is in my apartment watching us, and Elisia knows what she wants. And for whatever reason, she's comfortable with me. I place her hair behind her ear and see her for what she is, a gorgeous woman helping me move on. I put my lips on hers and she kisses me back. Our budding romance is forbidden now, and I don't care. It feels good to press my lips on hers.

I lie back on the couch, and she lies on top of me. We kiss for about an hour. Her hands feel my face, and I put my tongue in her mouth. I don't know what is going on between us, but our chemistry is undeniable. Elisia is still wrapped up in a blanket.

I pull away from her and start her bath for her, and she follows me. I hand her a towel and close the door. After the tub is full, I leave her alone.

"Thanks for everything Callum. I'm ready to move on now and try to be friends. I'm sure you'll make a great coach."

I kiss her one more time. I want to remember our happiness when we trained at the rink. My hands are all over Elisia. We've started up again, this chemistry between us could easily be addictive.

"You're welcome. Enjoy your bath, and I will make us some coffee. And thanks. I hope I can help you win competitions."

I close the door behind me and when I do Coach Ping calls me. The coffee grinds are everywhere, and I feel clumsy after kissing Elisia. Clumsy and jittery, like maybe I am falling for her a little too. But she asked me to kiss her one more time, and now that it's over between us, I am sad.

I've gotten used to her blonde hair resting against my chest. Now I am her coach, and our chemistry needs to be put aside. I will be spending all this time with her, and in the end, it won't mean anything. Because we both know how this will go. She will have tryouts with a new skater, and he will be far younger than me. Eventually, they will fall for each other, and I will be too late. Because by the time I actually fall for her, she will have moved on and will be in love with someone else.

"Callum, good news. All fifty try-out slots have been filled. When they saw your name was attached as a coach, they filled up so quickly. You are a celebrity. Isn't it wonderful?"

Coach Ping has no idea that the woman I am supposed to coach lies naked taking a bath in my bathtub. Just the thought makes me blush for some reason and not even I can explain it. Pretty soon I will be witnessing Elisia try out with fifty men, and I don't think I will ever be ready for that.

Bruno (Elisia's POV)

Callum is going to coach me; I don't know how to feel about that. Our chemistry will be hard to deny, but the only man who I will be allowed to get close to with be my new partner. It's sweet that they set up these tryouts for me. I love pair skating more than single skating. Being an equal match on ice and being in rhythm with another human being of the opposite sex, is fire. Derek set us on fire, if I skated with Callum, we could be legends. But he's chosen to coach me which is the next best thing.

Why did I ask Callum to kiss me? And why did he kiss me back? He didn't hesitate, he just kissed me, and I think he wanted to mean it too. He holds back when we kiss, he holds onto Ginger and the ghost of their love. I should visit her graveside with him, we still haven't been there yet, and I don't think he will ever be truly ready to let her go. At some point, I will have to either fight for what Callum and I have or let him go forever.

I leave Callum's apartment on a full stomach. We didn't talk much after I got out of the bath. He was a gentleman of course and gave me privacy. It feels wrong to borrow Ginger's clothes all the time. I really should give them back to him. They after all are a totem to what he has left of her.

"I'll see you at the arena in a few hours and thanks for setting up the tryouts with Coach Ping. I can't believe all fifty slots filled up that quickly."

"I'm not. Just look at you," Callum whispers to himself. But I know what he means and it's nice to receive a small compliment.

"What about me?"

"You're gorgeous, Elisia. Any skater would be lucky to be paired with you. I'll see you at the arena."

I instantly blush which is embarrassing enough considering I am blonde. My yellow hair and red cheeks make the rest of my face appear pink.

"Thanks, Callum. I'll see you at the arena then." He waves goodbye and the fire between us weakens. I don't want it to grow dim. I want to remember how he makes me feel. But he will never be free of her. Not really.

A few hours go by and with it the anticipation to get this try-out session over with. It sounded like a good idea at first but now I hate the idea. Fifty men prepared to skate with me and among them a stowaway.

"Derek, what are you doing here? This tryout is for people I actually might want to skate with. I don't know how to tell you this, but your name isn't on the list and for a good reason."

"Give me another chance, babe. We could be great together," Derek smirks as the flavor of throw-up appears on my tongue.

"Are you harassing my student? I believe she asked you to leave. It's time for you to go," Callum says as he puts his hand on my shoulder. His hand makes my skin burn and long for him to touch me in other ways. But I must put a lid on it and become a professional for the tryout to go on.

"I'll have the office team escort, Derek, out of the arena for you. Go get on the ice, Miss Algora," Callum says.

When he calls me 'Miss Algora' it shows that he is serious about closing the gaps between us. He is turning the page on our relationship. Building a bridge will make it harder for us to explore what we could mean to each other, and I don't know what Callum wants from me.

"Okay, Coach O'Leary. See you when it's over." Calling him coach is hard. I've tasted him on my lips and this forbidden student-teacher dynamic that we share makes this even harder. He looks at my lips and I blush.

"First up is, Jared Young," Coach Ping yells. The music fades and I step onto the ice. Jared lifts me a few times, but his height is rather short and it is clear that this isn't going to work out for me.

By the fifteenth man, I am convinced we will never find someone for me to skate with.

"Number sixteen is Mark Swenson." Mark is handsome but his use of style and flare prove his narcissistic tendencies.

My feet ache from being lifted by different hands. I will never find a partner. I stare at Callum, if only he would step out onto the ice. I would love to be lifted into the air by his hands. He's been nothing but kind to me, I hardly know him, and yet I trust him completely. Mother was right, I get involved too quickly and care too deeply. My legs hurt as we make our way into the mid-thirties of the auditions.

"Number thirty-five, Bruno Saunders."

Bruno is a tall handsome half-Italian stallion. I could easily be lifted into the air by him. He lifts me effortlessly and I blush slightly. I look back at Callum, who appears a bit jealous. Maybe Bruno is the man I need to pair with after all. Bruno kisses my cheek, and it sets Callum on edge. Coach Ping is too busy with the list of tryout names to notice.

After the last competitor is done. We thank them for appearing on the ice.

"Thank you, everyone, we will get back to you soon with the top three choices. Have a good weekend," Coach Ping says.

"Goodbye, Bella," Bruno says as he blows air kisses at me. The flattery from Bruno is winning me over, as well as Coach Ping.

"That Bruno seems to like you a lot. And he is perfect at lifting you into the air. He was so effortless when he did that. What do you think, Coach Callum?" Coach Ping asks.

"I don't like him. He's a brown noser. There is nothing good about him."

"Oh, Callum don't be so petty. He was one of the best skaters with Elisia today. In the end, it's her decision."

Callum doesn't say anything, he bites his lips. I can tell that skating with Bruno is going to annoy Callum or make him jealous.

"Well, it's no competition really. I have decided I want to skate with Bruno."

Coach Ping smiles and Callum rolls his eyes and crosses his arms. He needs to be a little jealous, it might be good for him. I only hope we can still be friends when all of this training is over because we both know I have chosen Bruno to test Callum O'Leary and it's nice to know my plans are already working.

Jealousy (Callum's POV)

I'm not jealous. No matter how smartass Bruno is, he really is the best skater of the fifty skaters who just auditioned. There is no way around it, I am going to have to watch Bruno touch every inch of Elisia's waist during practice. Why does that bother me so much? What is happening to me, Ginger?

"Coach Callum, is it okay with you if I am partnered with Bruno," Elisia asks, as I try not to show the truth that it bothers me.

"Sure. Let him know that he is the winner of the tryouts. Post it on social media Coach Ping it has been decided."

Coach Ping waves at me and asks me to follow her back to the arena offices. The offices in the back have several doors within the hallways.

"Step into my office, Coach Callum. We need to have a little chat."

I close the door behind me, unsure of what I have done. It's like I am back in high school all over again and Coach Ping is Principal Hanson.

"I need to ask you something and I need to know the truth right here, right now."

I hate the way Coach Ping makes me feel like I have done something wrong.

"What question do you need to ask me, Coach Ping?"

"Are you and Elisia involved in any way? I've seen the way you look at her. And it makes me wonder if this is going to be like Ginger all over again. I told you then what I am about to repeat now. Don't fall for a partner or student, dangerous things can happen if you do."

"Seriously, Coach Ping that's what you called me into your office for? I of all people know how dangerous romance and an ice accident can be. Do I have a relationship with Elisia, absolutely not. She and I are nothing but professionals. Are we done here? What a waste of my time."

"Callum, I know you find her, attractive."

"So do all the other fifty men who auditioned today. I am her coach, nothing more. I am still in love with Ginger, and she isn't alive anymore. I don't know what you want from me. I'll see you at practice and we can sort this out then. Goodbye, Coach Ping."

Maybe I don't sound convincing. But I need Coach Ping to leave matters of the heart alone for once. She has been too involved in my personal life in the past. I can handle Elisia. We have decided to keep our relationship strictly professional. I trust her to do the same back at me. No matter how jealous I am of Bruno or how jealous I might become. That part of our lives is over and it's time for all of us to move on before someone gets hurt.

"Callum wait it's not just that. I want you to be safe. I am just looking out for you. Don't you see that?"

Instead of walking away in anger, I take a deep breath. I turn to face Coach Ping.

"Yes, I do. But there is nothing to tell you about. She and I are just...friends."

I walk away probably not sounding convincing enough. But it's done and over with. There is no point in dwelling on what might have been between us. It was nice to think that for a single moment, happiness might have been mine. But fairy tales don't exist, and they certainly never will for me.

I head out of the arena. Bruno is showing off his muscles to Elisia. By now it's all-over social media that Elisia Algora and Bruno Saunders are being coached under Coach Ping and myself. I need to be level-headed and show Elisia that I am as mature as I claim to be. I need to set an example for her, as an older man I need to do the right thing and let her go and be young with someone her own age.

"Coach Callum, do you have a minute?" Bruno smirks.

His muscles retract and his biceps disappear. His long hair is tied back in a man bun. If his locks were down, he would have long flowing wavy black hair. His brown eyes show the testosterone in his veins, and I am not in a place to challenge him.

"Yes, do you need help with something?" Trying to sound like a teacher is exhausting work.

"Yes, I could use some advice on how to get with the ladies. We all know you dated your pair skating partner. So, what's the big secret?"

Bruno is asking me how to ask Elisia out. I can't even handle this; I can hardly contain my annoyance or my jealousy. This is all so stupid, why did I have to go and kiss her? That was so pathetic.

"Just ask her to go to a restaurant and let her pick," I reply.

I can't indicate my jealousy or anything, to do so would end my time with her. I told her I took this job to get to know her and I meant it. Ginger's ghost is telling me not to give up on this girl.

"Oh thanks, Coach. I will see if that works. I can't wait to get started it's going to be fun learning from a legend."

But the truth is I still haven't stepped onto the ice since Ginger fell. Coaching them means I will have to get back out there. Maybe I won't compete, but I will sharpen my blades and skate like I once did.

"Elisia, do you have a moment," I ask.

"Is everything alright, Callum?"

"I was wondering if you could meet me here at midnight. I need a little help with something."

She smiles and agrees. She doesn't know that I need her help finding my way back on the ice.

"And don't forget to bring your skates. I need to work with you a bit more." She agrees and Bruno continues to touch her shoulder. He whispers something in her ear and that belly laugh coming from her lips should be from something I say, not something that Bruno whispers. It takes all of my energy not to go over there and stop my new student from hitting on my female student. Instead, I walk away with a large piece of gum between my angry teeth.

Back on Ice (Elisia's POV)

"Do you want to get dinner with me," Bruno asks loudly for the whole arena to hear. It's not that I want to move on from Callum, but we agreed to be professional. And going on a date with and getting to know Bruno seems like something I should be pursuing.

"Sure, maybe we can eat at Olive Garden." Bruno smiles and puts his hand on my shoulder. His fingers are like long thick sausages, and they are callused a bit. Whereas Callum has softer hands.

I just need to think of Callum as my coach and maybe try to date Bruno eventually. It happens to most pair skaters, you either date, kiss, or mess around with your partner at least once before the big competition. Callum has made it clear that he is emotionally unavailable and is still in love with Ginger, the ghost that haunts his apartment. It might do him some good if he sold all of her belongings and got out of that apartment. But it's not my place to think about Callum or to get too attached.

"Sure, and maybe I can use my nose and pass a meatball over to you like that dog from that old Disney movie."

I pretend that his *Lady and the Tramp* reference is cute. It was endearing but not funny by any means. Callum's eyes appear sad as he walks away from the arena.

"Why are you staring at Coach Callum?" Bruno asks like a jealous boyfriend. But it's obvious that I was looking at him.

"I'm concerned about him. He's been down a lot lately pining away for his former skating partner."

"Well, don't concern yourself with him right now. We need to focus on training and getting to know each other if you know what I mean."

Bruno winks at me through his large thick bushy eyelashes. His lashes are larger than mine with mascara on them. His testosterone levels are off the charts, and I bet the girls back home would pine away for him.

He's handsome in his own way, but I am not taken by him. Callum's the one I can't stop thinking about and I hardly know either of them.

"Shall I drive us to Olive Garden then?" Bruno asks and I swear he's lowered his voice by a note or two to impress me. Needless to say, I am anything but impressed or amused. He's shallow, as the three-foot-end of a swimming pool. I want this date to go well, but I don't even know if I should consider it a date.

"Sure, let's split a large spaghetti and a basket of breadsticks," I say exhausted from the emotions in my heart.

I go on social media and see old pictures of Callum and Ginger plastered all over social media. They are retelling his Ginger story over and over, I hope he doesn't go on social media later today. The news of him returning to skating is big news and our photos will soon be everywhere in the skating world.

"That Ginger chick was hot. Too bad she died though. I hope Coach Callum has been on the ice since she died, you know?"

Is that why he wants to see me later tonight? Maybe Bruno isn't a dumb brute after all, maybe there are brains between that brawny exterior after all.

"Yeah, maybe," I reply.

We get out of the car and make our way inside the Olive Garden. I get to know Bruno and that he is a second-generation Italian. But at the end of the date, I am glad I got to know Bruno. He's a lot smarter than I originally thought.

"Thanks for taking me out tonight, Bruno I had a really good time. Maybe we can do this again some other time." I know it sounds like I am hoping for another date and maybe I am given that Callum is only my coach now, nothing more.

"Do you have time to go to a movie?" Bruno asks, trying to make the date last longer. It's only 7 pm and Callum asked me to meet him at 10 pm. I am sure I can squeeze it in.

"Sure, I have time. I have somewhere I need to be at ten. So, it can't be too long of a movie. What did you have in mind?"

"Maybe a Disney movie then. We can see Turning Red. It's about a girl who turns into a red panda," Bruno says.

He's clearly a Disney fan and so I am really. There's nothing wrong with belting out Moana songs at figuring skating practice.

"Sure, let's do it."

The date continues and I am antsy to get it over with. During the movie, Bruno decided to hold my hand and I let him. I wasn't happy about it, but it wasn't a marriage commitment. But it didn't feel right, it didn't feel like an inner spark existed. Despite his talent at skating and his grace with lifts, I don't know if this partnership will work out. But I have decided on Bruno and there is no one else available.

The movie ends and Bruno takes me back to my car. I drive away before he can kiss me. I can't let Bruno do that just yet. Maybe if Callum and I didn't work out in the end, Bruno will be the one.

I meet Callum alone in the parking lot of the civic arena. The rink is empty, and the lights are out. Callum waves at me and I jog toward him excited to see him standing there. My heart races when he smiles at me, it's a shame that I have fallen for my skating coach. It's a one-sided attraction, what's a girl to do? Nothing that's what.

He spins the keys around his finger and then unlocks the doors. I tuck my skates under my arm and follow him inside. Our breath echoes within the walls of the building. Without others to make it busy and loud, it is a quiet emptiness. An endless void in which my heartbeats will give me away and my crush on Callum will be revealed. He already knows about my crush, but I have to put it aside and pretend there is nothing there.

"Why am I here, Callum?" I ask as I put my skates on. My white skates are slightly dirty from the tryouts we had earlier.

"I need your help. I haven't been on ice since Ginger died. And I don't have the guts to look foolish in front of Coach Ping. Take my hand."

Callum looks at his feet and hesitates. His skates haven't made contact with the ice.

"I'll go first, and you can meet me in the middle." I skate toward the center and extend my arms out wide. The speed of my skates makes the air hit my face like a gentle breeze.

"Your turn, Callum. Look at me and only me." I have become his lighthouse guiding him through his inner storm. His skate touches the ice, and his knees wobble.

Callum turns on a song on his phone and plays it loudly. It's a salsa. He grabs my hand and has magically made his way to the center.

"Let's see what you've got," Callum says beneath his breath.

Callum's size is even better than Bruno's. We got to be great together on the ice. We could be legends; he takes my hands and it's at this second, I know I am going to fall hard for him. The thought makes me blush, but I focus on the task at hand...helping Callum gain his inner confidence.

Our hands touch and he spins me and twirls me around the ice. It's intense and sexy. The salsa beat picks up and it's as if Callum never stopped skating. He lifts me effortlessly. He avoids any hard or advanced moves. Because if he did, he would get jitters and lose his focus.

He ends our practice with a death spiral. He is the anchor spinning in a circle and I am practically lying on the ice as we pivot in a perfect circle. He pulls me in, and the song ends.

I've never experienced this much chemistry on the ice. It's intoxicating and I promised myself I would behave. But this verifies everything I think and feel about myself. That my crush won't be able to be cast aside and no matter what I do, I will like Callum a lot.

My face is red, and I don't hide it or deny it. I don't care anymore. He deserves to see the way he makes me feel.

"Good job, Callum. I am so proud of you for being able to skate with me tonight. I am glad I could help you. Ginger would be proud of you too."

He smiles at me, and I want him to wrap his arms around me and kiss me. But it's not realistic. We are just two professionals now. Student and teacher. And that's the way it will stay and that is going to eat me up inside. I only hope Callum will remember this night for a long time to come.

"Let's do this again sometime," he says. And I quickly agree with him, because this is the only way we will get alone time together and I am not about to let that go. I smile at him, and we head back to the bleachers and remove our skates. His smile tells me everything, that he is happy, and for a moment that smile is from me and not Ginger. That is something I will never forget either.

Being Professional Sucks (Callum's POV)

Elisia turns to skate away from me. But before she can leave, I turn another song on for us to skate to. I know that turning this on is an invitation for her to stay, but she's given me my wings back. By agreeing to meet me tonight, she's agreed to give me hope and a little bit of my confidence has been restored.

"I don't understand. Aren't we done? Did you need to practice some more?"

Being professional sucks, our intensity on the ice brings me back to what I miss about Ginger. It's just her and I and no one else judging us. I wouldn't be able to skate without her by my side. Maybe I could skate again if she let me lead her and show her off. But I can't show her off and show everyone how amazing she is. She's my student and I am her coach, that role of partner has been given to Bruno Saunders. Just the thought of him makes me jealous and mad. When I'm not in coach mode I can admit to myself that I'm jealous down to my bones.

"No, we don't need to practice more. I just want to skate with you a little while longer. If you're comfortable." I blush a little when I speak, and trying to hide it from her is foolish. We are past hiding things, and yet we do for some reason.

She blushes and I can tell she has enjoyed this as much as I have. I hold out my hand to her and she takes it. The violin from the song plays slowly in the background and the cello comes in a minute later. It's a sad duet piece about two lovers who can't be together. The instrumental music continues, and I skate with her. We spin at the same time and land our jumps at the same time. With more training, we could compete together. Our chemistry is undeniable but also forbidden.

She's as talented as Ginger and her skating mannerisms take me back to yester year when I was on top of the world. I used to be an amazing skater, could Elisia make me feel that high again? The high only an audience can bring me.

According to my contract, I am not allowed to give private lessons after hours and I am also not allowed to fraternize with my students. But we were way past that before I signed anything. The song ends and I lift her on my legs. It's the only lift I am comfortable doing. Anything else will remind me of failure and everything I lost.

I want to hold her here forever. The feeling of her hips in my hands as we glide across the ice gives me power and joy. It's terrifying and dangerous. It's high and it's low. It's erotic and we both know we have feelings for each other.

The song ends and I lean Elisia back on my arm. Would it be wrong to kiss her? I told her we would be professional, and I meant it. I wish I hadn't, for this moment would be perfect. She helped me find my way back to the ice, and that is something I am grateful for. To love her would be wrong, to break my contract further would be wrong.

Her smile makes me hold her there a little while longer. She puts her hands around my neck, and she kisses me instead. My heart leaps out of my chest, and I kiss her back. I kiss every inch of her lips. I put my tongue in her mouth and moan with delight at her beauty. I pull away startled by my actions.

"Don't look at me like that. I kissed you because I wanted to, Callum. Want to know the secret? I enjoyed every bit of it. I won't kiss you again though, I know you want to be professional," Elisia says as she backs away from me.

"Yes, we should be professional. But for what it's worth, I... kissed you back and I enjoyed it too. And thanks for helping me find my way back on the ice again. I couldn't have done it without you."

We both skate back toward the seats. And we take our skates off. I turn the lights out in the rink and follow Elisia into the hallway. The silence is awkward. Our feet echo in the hallways and my sneakers squeak across the floor.

"Are we even capable of being professional around each other, Callum? We seem to give in to our...attractions. If you really mean it then I will back off, if you need me to be professional, I really am capable of it. Maybe you don't believe me. Just tell me what it is you want," Elisia says as her eyes turn red.

"Let me think about it. I need time to think about it. In the meantime, want to meet me back here tomorrow night?"

Elisia smiles and her red eyes become white again. She's sensitive and anything I say will harm or help her. I don't know what she might see in a man like me, but I am not going to end things badly with her tonight. After all she's the reason my skates touched the ice tonight. She's the reason my heart pounded, and I fell in love with ice again. Her hips beneath my hands during those lifts were intense and I would give anything to show her off to an audience.

"Yes, I would love to spend more time on the ice with you."

She starts to walk out the door and I stop her. I put my thumb on her face and touch her bottom lip. When I close my eyes to kiss her, she's already placed her lips on mine. Whatever is going on between us is mutual, and I think we've just agreed to keep it a secret.

Student and Teacher (Elisia's POV)

Being professional is stupid. I know now that by day Callum is my coach and at night it might be different. When I get to the rink everyone is gossiping about me and Bruno. They have already made us an item, but no one suspects that Coach Callum's lips have tasted mine.

"Good afternoon, Elisia. You look tired. Were you up all night thinking about me," Bruno asks as I hurry up to greet him.

I haven't thought about him at all actually. If I wasn't distracted by Callum, I might have taken an interest in Bruno. He is a kind man from what I can tell. The center of all the gossip might have made his ego larger though.

"Hi, Bruno. What's going on? Why does everyone look so angry," I ask. The tension in the arena grows heavy and I don't know what the reason is.

"Skaters and coaches this way, please. We have a crisis we need to address. Everyone let's make this quick and sit on the seats in the rink," Coach Ping says.

Coach Ping looks angry with her arms crossed and her eyes going back and forth between her watch and Callum. An office manager hands Coach Ping a megaphone. So, we can all hear her speak loudly in the back row.

"We have a cheater in our midst. You have all signed contracts with the arena that when these doors are closed you will not practice and get more ice time. Running this place costs money and using it without permission is a liability issue. I am too tired to run a full investigation right now. But I want everyone to look out and see the skate marks on the ice. To the skaters who made those tracks last night after hours, this is your final and only warning. If I find any more skating tracks on my rink and find the skaters responsible, you will not be allowed to compete or take lessons within these walls ever again. I hope everyone understands. Dismissed," Coach Ping says.

Coach Ping looks straight at me like she knows it was Callum and me. I can't risk seeing him tonight. It wouldn't be right. He needs this job, and my career isn't over yet. I don't want to throw in the towel for romance, but it's the only alone time I will get with Callum. I would rather see him on the ice and act professional, than not see him at all. I couldn't bear to not see him. This whole situation is tricky and sucks.

"Well, we know it wasn't us Elisia. It was clearly a pair skating couple and we were at Olive Garden. Whoever they are they need to stop. I feel bad for that couple, how the hell did they get in here anyway? Maybe they broke a window," Bruno asks.

The more he opens his mouth the more I realize he might be right, that no one will suspect me if Bruno tells them all we weren't here and those are pair skating tracks, I might be off the hook after all. I touch my lips and think of Callum, last night was the last time I will hang out with him in person for a while.

"Coach Callum, you got a second?" I ask trying to pretend that what he shared last night meant nothing.

"Yeah, hi Elisia. What's going on?"

"About last night, I think it's best if we lay low for a while. I don't want you getting fired over me. So can we pause whatever this is for a while and maybe when the competition is over, we can try again," I ask knowing that I am wishing for the impossible.

What I am asking for is completely unrealistic. We keep going back and forth between friends with benefits to professionals. It's exhausting work.

"Yes, I am thinking the same thing. I do appreciate your help. I am confident I can teach you both properly now. If you want to come over to my place later this evening, I won't stop you," Callum replies with a flirtatious eagerness in his voice.

"No, Callum. We need to stop this before it gets started. I'm sorry. Please give me space. I can't give up skating for this," I say as I point to the space between us.

I know I've hurt Callum, but I've hurt myself even more. I never thought I'd have to choose between two things that I care about, and it isn't fair, no it isn't fair at all.

"I understand. From now on we are just student and teacher. I feel nothing for you, and you feel nothing for me. This hasn't been easy for me you know. Trying to let Ginger go to be with you. But thanks for making my decision easier. You won't have to wait for a competition to be over with to make this work, because I am telling you now there will be nothing for you to come back to. I can't wait and wait; I can't go back and forth. Maybe you can, but I can't. And before this gets any further, I'm ending it permanently. You have your career and I have mine. We are professionals, nothing more. See you on the ice, Elisia," Callum says as he walks away and gives me the cold shoulder.

I know he's right, that this world of skating is both beautiful and cruel. We both want each other too much, but the dynamics of our careers have made it impossible. My emotions get the better of me, and I cry as he walks away. Bruno approaches and has no idea why I am crying.

"Are you okay? What did Coach Callum say to make you so upset," Bruno asks. I don't say anything, I just let Bruno hug me as I cry next to him in the arena cafe.

The Professional (Callum's POV)

I'm angry and upset, I am blown off by a woman I barely know and haven't even dated. It's my fault for not erasing our skate tracks on the ice. I should have used the Zamboni to hide our tracks. How was I supposed to know our little night of flirting would involve Coach Ping and an almost witch hunt? If I don't bring up the skate tracks on the ice to Coach Ping, I am sure I will be off the hook.

"Coach Callum, a word in private," Coach Ping says with a lowered voice.

"Yeah, what's going on," I say playing coy. If I play along maybe someone else can take the blame for a little while until I fess up later. I'm still about to be scolded like a little boy in grade school.

"Who do you think it was last night that got more skate time?"

"Maybe that Derek guy who used to be engaged to Elisia? He has a motive to get her in trouble. He's heartbroken and tried to be involved in her tryouts and got rejected." I shrug my shoulders in the air and my hands gesture with them. Placing the blame on Derek is a cowardly move, but I need this money. This money means I get a roof over my head.

"That's a good point, Callum. Well, if it happens again, I will know who to interrogate first. Any idea how Elisia and Bruno are getting along? Did she say how their date went last night," Coach Ping asks seeing if I can handle this conversation.

I know he asked her on a date, but I didn't realize she accepted his invitation. And then had the nerve to skate with me alone after-hours last night. What an idiot I've become, well never again. What was I thinking letting Elisia into my corner of the world? She's young and has Bruno, I'm an old has been and no amount of skating with a beauty like Elisia will ever change that.

"Pretty well, I'd say. I think he asked her on a date last night. Sounds like she accepted, good for them," I say while biting down on the insides of my cheeks. My jaw is going to hurt from the jealousy I feel inside.

My gums are raw and chewing later will be painful. But maybe Elisia is worth all of this heartache and confusion. She got me back onto the ice and I am grateful for that, if nothing else came from our hangout.

"Well get on the ice and show these amateurs what real skating looks like. You are ready to skate again, right Callum?"

"Yes, of course, I am. Ginger would want me to make a life for myself and to be happy with something again."

Being happy is an illusion for the uneducated. We are told the more money you have the happier you will become. I won all the skating awards and pairing trophies and had tons of money as a result. But none of that matters, because I was only rich when Ginger was pregnant, and we were about to start our lives together as a little family.

"Glad to hear it. Go get them, Coach Callum."

Up until last night, I didn't have the courage to skate. But thanks to Elisia I found my wings, but she clipped them by rejecting me. She stands in the middle of the rink beside Bruno. He even smells like a dumb brute from here, it's a good thing he isn't an asshole like Elisia's ex, Derek.

I skate toward the center to where Elisia is and only tune in on her. We begin our lesson and Bruno holds her hands. They push and pull each other across the rink, and I blow my whistle a few times giving Bruno advice. Ten minutes into the lesson we are interrupted by Derek.

"Hello, Elisia. Over here. Hey, I want to show you, someone. I have found a new pair skating partner, and I think you might want to see who it is."

I young brunette woman about twenty comes waltzing in with green leggings on. She's well-built and is a bit shorter in height than Elisia.

When Elisia turns to look at her replacement, she gets flustered.

"Hello, Elisia. Yeah, I am back, and this season is going to be tougher than you think it is," the brunette mystery woman says.

"Look, I don't know who you are, but we are in the middle of a lesson. So if you don't mind, " I say.

"Who the hell is this, hottie? Oh, where are my manners, my name is Jeka Provost." She waves to us obnoxiously from the sidelines.

"I'm Coach Callum O'Leary. And I think it's time for you to go. Coach Ping see them out please."

Elisia looks scared and shaken. Jeka must be her skating rival. We all have that one person on the ice who is just as good or a little bit better than us, who pushes us to win.

"Elisia, are you going to be okay," Bruno asks. For some reason, Bruno taking an interest in her both annoys me and liberates me. I only wish I was the one to ask her first.

Elisia nods and continues the lesson without talking. She shakes and nods her head and clears her throat. And before I know it the lesson is over. Elisia and I won't be spending time together later and it looks like Bruno has already jumped into his new role of befriending the woman he will now call his partner. Too bad I didn't take her up on the offer when I had the chance. How was I supposed to know that skating with her would feel like home? And now I have let her go for the betterment of the competition and professionalism's sake.

More than Friends (Elisia's POV)

I've skipped a week of practice. Bruno understands that I need my space for my mental health. Between being taunted by Derek, Jeka returning as the ghost of Christmas past, and Callum's cold shoulder, I can't take it.

I have ordered more door dashes this week than I care to admit. It's a good thing I can work remotely and still afford this apartment. My parents are both dead, but it was their dying wish for me to keep skating. Coach Ping still owes me money for recruiting Callum back to the ice. I knew he had it in him to return, he only had to believe in himself to get there.

There's no comfort in skating for me anymore. My skating role model can't even give me comfort. I used to look up to Ginger from afar, she was perfect like Michelle Kwan on landings, and as graceful as Tessa Virtue during pairs events. She was flawless and captivated an audience. But now she reminds me of Callum, the man I can't have but see every day to train. I took this week off for myself. Maybe it's selfish but we all need to be selfish a little bit at times to help find our center.

Callum lost his way, and I brought him back to the light. Who is going to be my beacon of hope? With the return of Jeka Provost, I am terrified. She was always a little more talented than me, and Derek knew that. But I never thought he would seek her out to psyche me out during a pairs lesson.

I remember when we were thirteen, Jeka and I had the same coach. They would forbid us from being friends, we were nothing but competition, growing up alongside our rivals. Our nails mattered, our dresses mattered, and our individualism was stripped away. I wanted to be her friend, and she wanted that too for a moment. Until the medals came out and she always got first, and I was always second best to her.

Always in second by half a second or less. Our scores were almost the same, but never enough for me to be the victor. And if she knew that

I liked Callum even a little, she could win him over, and then I really would be in second place to her in every aspect of my life. She's in my head and has been since I was that little scared young teen competing at thirteen-years-old. I wanted a friend and she wanted to brag that I was never going to be good enough to go to the Olympics.

I've been in sweatpants for days sulking. I'm allowed to sulk and play dumb computer games. The door rings and I quickly put on my T-shirt and put my hair in a bun.

"Who is it," I ask.

"It's Callum, can we talk?" Why is Callum here at my apartment? I look awful, I can't let him see me like this, or maybe I can since we aren't even a thing. But why am I so flustered by him, do I even like him that much?

"Sure, come in I apologize for how I look and how my apartment looks. I haven't been myself this week."

He sits down on my couch, and I want to cry that he came to check up on me.

"Would you like some coffee or tea?"

"No, I bought you some coffee actually. I've come here to level with you. The other day we said some things to each other, and I don't know what I am saying. But I guess I didn't mean some of those hurtful things I said. I must be the reason you have decided to quit skating. I've already spoken with Coach Ping and if the only way you will return to the ice is if I am no longer your coach, then I will step down if that would convince you to return."

My mouth opens at the mere shock of his suggestion. This whole week he thought he was the reason for my skating absence. It's hard to face him, but I am scared of Jeka mostly. She's the main reason.

"No, don't do that Callum. And what exactly did you tell Coach Ping about us?"

"Oh, nothing. I just told her you might do better with a female coach instead of someone...like...me." He plays with his hands and picks at a scab on his thumb.

"You're cute when you're..." I start blushing I didn't mean to blurt it out. But he is cute when he is trying to be a gentleman.

"So, you think I'm cute now?" His smirk returns to his face, and I've missed it.

"Callum, you know what I meant. Weren't we going to be professional about how we treat each other from now on?" This back-and-forth we have is unhealthy and exciting at the same time.

"I'm sorry, you're right. I guess I just can't help it with you sometimes. I get cared away, because...I miss being needed by someone. That probably sounds stupid. You don't need me at all, do you? Sorry, I don't mean to waste your time," Callum says while blushing. I've seen him blush, but this is different, this is a full-on embarrassment from his head to his toes.

He stands up and hands me the coffee he bought me. He gets ready to leave and I grab his hand. I don't care anymore about being professional, I just can't anymore.

"What if I want you to waste my time? And you're wrong it's not stupid to want to be needed. And I do Callum I need you around. What if I want to be your friend? What if I want to get to know you better? Is that so wrong?"

I can't hold back anymore, I just can't. I'm on the edge of the couch, begging- hoping that he understands that I need him. I can't skate without him. I can't breathe without knowing he is taken care of.

"No, it's not wrong," he says as he sits back down. He puts my loose strand of blonde hair behind my ear and pulls me in for a hug.

"Thank you, Elisia. It's nice to have a real friend again. I haven't had any real friends, since Ginger died."

When he pulls away from me our foreheads touch, and we still haven't crossed back into the land of unprofessional. But we both want to, it's just a game of who will give in first and I am determined for it not to be me this time.

"Are we just friends though? I get confused about us. We keep going back and forth, and I try to do what you say. I try to be professional and keep my thoughts to myself."

"That's how skating is. The World of skating has rules that need to be followed. I'm not supposed to like you, Elisia. But I do, I really do. And tonight, I want to put that aside and..." He takes a deep breath, the words he is saying make my heart pound.

"Tonight, I want to be more than just...friends." He pulls me in and leans in to kiss me and when he does my cell phone rings. It's Coach Ping.

"Excuse me, Callum. It's Coach Ping." I'm frustrated, we were having a heart-to-heart conversation and Coach Ping has to interrupt us. I'll never have a moment alone with Callum. We live on thin ice, and that's the world of skating. We fight and we win trophies, but we don't fight for deep relationships...because they don't exist in our world.

"Hello, Coach Ping what's going on?"

"I'll tell you what's going on. We are a week short on training. And we have you to thank for that. If you don't come into practice, tomorrow consider yourself replaced. And as for paying you for recruiting coach Callum, you can forget it. If you ever want to skate in my rink again, come to your lesson tomorrow at noon and not a minute later. Are we clear?"

"Yes, Coach Ping. I understand. See you tomorrow," I reply.

Coach Ping is angry and hangs up the call as quickly as she dialed it. She's killed my mood and now I am not in the mood for romance with Callum.

Let Go (Callum's POV)

Elisia returns and by the look on her face, I can tell that it's my time to leave. We keep having moments together, but it's all words. We are either too hesitant, shy or in the wrong place at the wrong time.

"Elisia, I need to be heading out. I have a private lesson with Bruno this afternoon. But don't worry, we can pause this conversation and come back to it some other time. Enjoy the coffee."

I open the door and Elisia finds my hand again. I don't know how to convince her that I want to continue our conversation later when it makes sense. In all fairness, she didn't have to pick up the phone when Coach Ping called. Coach Ping has a habit of maintaining loyalty with guilt trips and fear. Ginger was above these manipulative tactics but not me. I could only lie to Coach Ping for a little while before it came back to haunt me.

"Can we ever have a private lesson again," Elisia asks as she folds her fingers into mine.

"Yes, I think we can. Want to meet at the rink at night again?"

"We can't, Callum. Coach Ping will definitely notice, and I am already on thin ice with her because I skipped a week."

"Why did you skip practice this week," I ask to drag out our goodbye.

"Because...Jeka's better than me. She's a childhood rival and I could never beat her," Elisia says while looking down at our hands.

"Don't worry you can do anything you put your mind to. And you still didn't answer my question. Do you want to meet after hours tonight we can ride in the Zamboni together when we are done?"

Her smirk tells me she is interested, and I kiss her on the cheek as I leave. We are on the fence between professionalism and liking each other. I could almost fall for her, but I can still feel Ginger's ghost judging me and telling me I am failing. How much of that is true and how much of that is the poison of my inner voice?

"Sure, that would be nice. If we can ride the Zamboni, then I am all in. I've never been on one actually," Elisia says.

I give her one more hug and decide not to kiss her. I want to spend the day thinking about if this is what I really want. Is this fair to her? Does our almost ten-year age gap even matter? Should I let Bruno have a chance at her?

I'm so scared of getting caught. It's like I am in high school all over again trying to hide my alcohol stash before my mom finds out. I haven't been this happy since Ginger died, that's good, right?

The time flies and the lesson with Bruno is upon me. He put dreadlocks in his hair since the last time we saw each other. He looks like an Italian pirate. My guess is he is going to try to win Elisia over. It's fun to watch knowing she and I are testing the waters in secret. I only hope she is not testing the waters with him behind my back too.

"Hey, Coach Callum. Sorry, I am late. Do you think Elisia will show up tomorrow? We are a week behind, and I tried to give her space, but it is getting weird."

"Yeah, she will be back. Coach Ping is looking into it."

"I heard you were looking into it too," Bruno says like I am being accused of something.

"What is that supposed to mean, Saunders?" I call him by his last name to remind him he is my student.

"Nothing Coach, I heard you stopped by her apartment."

I turn the music on and begin our lesson. Bruno's half-smile tells me that he is trying to piss me off. It's not good to piss a coach off during training, I might just make something look like an accident one of these days.

"Do you like her, coach," Bruno asks as our lesson ends.

"Like who?"

"Elisia? Do you like her? Some of the other guys think you might."

"She is my student. I am her teacher. That is quite the accusation, Saunders. Whoever these friends of yours are, I suggest you give them this message. What if these rumors don't stop then this arena will be forced to kick all males out of its program until the accuser steps forward. Are we clear, Saunders? Don't make me hold a meeting like we had the other day. Are you the secret skater who pair-skated on the ice after hours? You can fess up now or I can report you, either way, I would watch yourself if I were you. Especially around your coach, I have the power to make you or break you. You can go home now."

Bruno doesn't say anything to my backlash. I've defended myself and established our roles. I know I am the secret skater and that this makes me a hypocrite, but I had to push back and push back hard.

The night couldn't get here any faster. I stay at the arena and work. I pretend to get in my car and drive away like I have plans. But I don't I'm restless and am excited to see Elisia. She parks at the movie theater across the street and walks over. I let her in through the back. We don't say anything to each other, I've thought about her all day. She does mean something to me, maybe more than a little something.

We put our skates on and still haven't said anything to each other. I put the music on and we pick up where we left off.

"Let's make up a routine together like it's just you and me going to the competition. It could be fun."

We practice for two hours together. I lift her more and more each time the song starts over. But I am too scared to let go. The last time I let go of a woman on ice, I wasn't there in time, and I don't have it in me to ever do that ever again.

"Let go, Callum. I've got this. You have to trust me too. Let me catch myself. I know we can do it. I know you're scared but we can do harder lifts. Let me find my feet as you set me down. Just grab my hips and don't lift me too far off the ground."

She's right, it is about trust. If I don't trust her on ice what will that say about me if we ever get into a relationship? We have to push and pull each other like water against the shore. The moon makes the tides, and the ocean knows the shore is waiting for it. Just like Elisia knows her footwork. I put the music on, and we start with a synchronized lutz.

The music intensifies and I hold her hand as we practice the death spiral. It's my favorite move. It's the woman trusting the man to always be there like the sun being the center of the galaxy with the moon orbiting around it. When she is done orbiting around me, I put my hands on her hips and lift her into the air. I spin around and raise her higher and higher. I put her down gently.

The music stops and I meet her in the middle. I sit on my butt in the center, and she sits beside me. We both laugh at how much fun our pairing together has become.

"That was fun. I had an amazing time. Maybe we could do this again tomorrow night. Want to ride the Zamboni with me?"

Elisia skates next to me and we take off our skates together. She follows me to the Zamboni. I turn it on, it's been a while since I've done this but how hard can it be?

"Time to erase our tracks this time. Goodbye evidence," I say as loud as I can. My voice echoes on the rink. Elisia sits behind me and holds my waist as tight as she can. It takes me thirty minutes to delete our path in the ice.

"Wow, this thing is a lot slower than it looks," Elisia comments as she kisses my cheek. This is one of the best dates I've been on. I didn't know what happiness felt like, I thought it looked like Ginger. I didn't know happiness could look like other people too.

I park the Zamboni and help Elisia get down. She's smiling and looks as happy as I feel inside. Maybe we really could be happy together. I am not sure I am ready for a full-on relationship.

"Callum, there's something I want to tell you," she stops herself. And doesn't make eye contact with me.

"Yeah, sure what is it? Let me guess you enjoyed tonight as much as I did?"

"Yes, I did. I really did. It was great fun. But no, it's not just that. What I mean to say is...I think I'm..."

She stops and doesn't finish. Whatever it is she is trying to say is important.

"Is everything okay?"

"Yes. I think I'm falling in love with you," Elisia says as she covers her mouth immediately afterward.

I wasn't expecting her to say anything like that to me. I don't know how I feel yet. Sure, I could see myself getting to this point, but she's already more there than I am. If I don't do something she will hate herself, so I pull her hand aside and decide to kiss her.

I kiss her gentle lips. I don't know what to say to her, so instead, I just show her that she means something to me too. She knows my pain and that letting go of Ginger will be one of the hardest things I will ever have to do. And for now, showing her is more important than telling.

The Fakers (Elisia's POV)

Callum didn't say it back. Damn, I said it too early. Well, I didn't exactly say it. I said I think I am... but he did kiss me afterward. Why do I have to over-analyze this at six in the morning? If I don't get REM sleep before I see Coach Ping, she will think I am too lazy to be a student.

My dreams take me back to our date. It was sweet and perfect. Everything that I like about Callum happened last night. I don't want to push him over the edge. I don't want to mean more to him if it will never happen. He would be the perfect soul mate to have on and off the ice. Ginger was lucky enough to love him in his youth, and I'm the hyena living off his scraps.

I wake up with hardly any time to get ready for practice. I clean my blades a bit and head out the door. This time no one will know about our time on the ice.

The arena is noisy and the silence from last night is missed. It was only Callum and I and our voices stretching across the ice. Now it is laughter, coaches clapping, and skates scraping the ice. Coach Ping waves at me and opens her mouth.

"Hi, Elisia. So nice of you to join us. What made you change your mind?"

"My loyalty to you of course," I say knowing that buttering her up is the only way anymore.

"Good girl, and don't you forget it. Oh, and I have a check for you for recruiting Coach Callum. I don't know what methods you have been using on him but keep up the good work and I might buy you new skates."

I don't want to be Coach Ping's pawn anymore. She wanted me to recruit Callum back to the rink. If he ever finds out he will think I made up the whole thing. But I didn't I couldn't make up feelings for him.

It's just not possible. His short brown wavy hair and happy expression are from last night. I gaze at him as I pretend to listen to Coach Ping.

"Elisia, who are you staring at," Coach Ping asks with a viper in her throat.

I quickly look at Bruno and blow him a kiss to cover my mistake. If she saw that it was Callum who made me this happy, she wouldn't let him coach me anymore. Unfortunately for me, Callum saw the kiss and rolled his eyes.

"Don't fall for your partner just yet. Wait until later. You need to focus on your career and the competition. No dating. No boys. Are we clear? That includes... Coach Callum."

The sound of his name causes me to stumble and blush. I can't help myself. I could stare at him all day, but Coach Ping found out. How? We were so discreet.

"Coach Callum? Ha-ha! Yeah, right like that would ever happen." I try to shake it off and try to deny it. I look at Bruno and blow another kiss.

"Oh, please I've been around long enough to know when a student and coach have been messing around. As long as you understand right here and now that it's over between you then I think you can continue being his student. If one hair is out of place, I will have him coaching Derek and Jeka. Are we clear?"

No, not again. I can't choose between Callum and skating. Or maybe I can. Maybe I can have both. I don't know anything anymore. But I am not confessing to her until I know it's not a trick.

"Seriously, why do you think I am into a coach? That would be pathetic. He's too old for me. In fact, I am going to ask Bruno to dinner."

"That's a much more preferable choice. Go ahead then, let's see you ask your man on a date," Coach Ping smiles like being with Bruno is what I want or desire. But since I don't have a choice.

I tiptoe over to Bruno and whisper something in his ear. I asked him to come over later to eat pizza at my house and watch a movie. Coach

Ping is still watching me, and for the sake of Callum's career I take one for the team, I pull Bruno in for a kiss, and our lips touch.

"I can't wait to see you tonight then," I say to Bruno as he kisses my cheek again. The worse part about pretending is doing it to protect someone you love. But for me having Callum watch my kiss with Bruno hurt like a thousand wasp stings and Coach Ping probably knows it.

I meet Callum on the ice. He doesn't look at me or say anything.

"Callum, can we talk? It's not what you think," I say.

"I don't know what you are talking about, Miss Algora. Go get your boyfriend and meet me back here in five minutes," Callum says as he puts earbuds in his ears and does laps around the rink.

My stomach hurts the way it used to when the acid would appear. The stomach acid from competition nerves. I always kept Pepto in my bag back then to help with moments like this. But I can't stop, the emotions are too much. I don't feel well. I need to drink water.

"Are you, okay Elisia? You don't look so good," Bruno says while taking my hand.

As he takes my hand on the rink, Callum passes by bumping Bruno's shoulder. I don't like him being cold to me. I did this to protect his job, to protect him. Because the only thing I love more than figure skating is Callum O'Leary and if I had to give up my skates and career to prove it, I know I would.

"Yes, I'm fine. Let's start our lesson." Callum is cold to me and only talks to Bruno. I'm not even worth his eye contact. But I did mean every word I said last night. I have fallen in love with Callum, and today I'm turning in my blades after class.

If You'll Let Me (Elisia's POV)

I can't face Coach Ping after all. I need a night to think about permanently quitting. If I go on a date with Bruno, it will make everyone think I am following the plan. The truth is there is no plan, there is no script telling me what to do next. It's all improv from this point on. I am making it up as I go just like a fiction writer does with their stories.

Our lives are like a book outline. We have some idea of how they might go, but the final outcome never matches the end result. There's nothing wrong with that, but for me giving up skating for Callum might be the right thing to do.

My date with Bruno is boring and predictable. He puts his arm around me and tries to grab my boob. I get up to pee to get away. Our hands touch in the popcorn bowl, and it feels like middle school. Middle school romance is too immature for me no matter how nice Bruno is, I want Callum. Bruno goes in for a kiss, and I pull away.

"I'm sorry, Bruno. I can't. It's...not you. It's just hard when I..." Bruno puts his hands on my lips.

"That's okay. I knew something was up with you today. I knew we weren't going to work out from the beginning. Not as a real couple, maybe as a pair skating couple sure."

"How did you know," I ask knowing it came out strong and forceful.

"Because you like Coach Callum. Or at least I think you do," he replies and finds my eyes.

How does everyone know that? Everyone but Callum that is. Isn't that always how it goes? The couple doesn't know, but everyone else around them gets annoyed they don't know.

"How did you, guess? Did Coach put you up to this?"

"No, no one did. I came back to the rink the other night after hours. And I saw you skating with him. You looked so happy. I left as soon as I could. But then I saw the music stop and I saw you kiss him. I didn't tell Coach Ping because she quite frankly scares the shit out of me. And if I told her she would know I was there after hours. So, I didn't say anything. Why did you kiss me then?"

Wow, Bruno is not only a good and loyal friend for not ratting me out, but he also cares.

"Coach Ping basically threatened to fire, Callum if I didn't date you. Sorry, but I had to do something to save his career. And you don't have to worry about covering for me because after today it's over between Callum and me. He doesn't think of me like that. I should have stopped this the first time we skated after hours."

"You've skated with him before? Are you trying to cheat in competition?"

"No, I was trying to help him conquer his fear of skating. If I didn't get him on the ice. He was going to let skating go forever. I'm the first person he has skated with since Ginger died. I thought I could help him let go of Ginger, but I can't. Her ghost haunts him, and I will never be her. So, I've decided to quit...skating. I'm afraid you will have to find a new partner."

"No, you're wrong. You can't give up skating. Although, I will need to find a new partner. You and Coach Callum on the ice were breathtaking. And I just don't say that about anyone. You have chemistry on and off the ice. I wouldn't be a good friend if I let you give up skating. Until you figure it out with Coach Callum and how you feel or not, you will train with me. I will push you hard and you will know what to do. I'll find another partner and maybe she will want to date me for real. And Elisia, no hard feelings about this date. It was quite fun, to be honest. I hope we can be friends when this is over?"

I smile at Bruno. If I wasn't in love with Callum, Bruno, in his own way, would be just as eye-catching. My eyes are red, I can't pick between skating and Callum. I can't do any of this anymore.

"I can't pick between Callum and skating. I thought I loved skating more than anything, but I don't."

My apartment door opens, and Callum lets himself in. I don't know why he is here or how much he might have overheard. My tears fall even more.

"Elisia, we need to talk...in private."

"You can't just come to my apartment while I am on a date and expect him to just leave because you demand him to," I yell.

Bruno laughs at the way we carry ourselves. But what am I supposed to do? I have feelings for Callum sure, but he is being an ass right now.

"It's okay Elisia. I was just leaving. Thanks for hanging out. I guess I'll see you both at practice tomorrow." Bruno leaves and winks at me when Callum isn't looking. He's so cheeky.

I shut the door and cross my arms. I'm annoyed Callum didn't listen to me at the rink. I'm annoyed he is here right now but also amused. Life is full of surprises, and I don't know what to say.

"Bruno is gone. What do you want Callum? Why should I listen to you when you ignored me at the rink?"

"You're the one who went on a date with Bruno tonight and kissed him. How was I supposed to feel? You cheated on me," Callum says as he crosses his arms and bites his cheeks.

"No, I didn't. We aren't even dating, Callum. And besides, it was a fake date...to get Coach Ping off my back about you."

"What are you talking about," Callum asks as his anger calms down slightly.

"Coach Ping was asking too many questions so I pretended to like Bruno so you wouldn't lose your job. But since you think I am so horrible; I've decided to leave it all behind. I don't even want to skate anymore. Tomorrow is my last day."

"Why the hell would you do that?"

"Because I love you, Callum. I'd rather be with you than be on ice. And I know I am not Ginger enough for you to hear that. That's on me. But I needed to tell you...once. So, there it's out there. I thought I loved skating more than anything, but then you happened. You made skating flirty and daring. You made me love you more than my skates. I wanted to get you back on the ice, but I didn't want to fall for you in the process. That wasn't in the cards for me. But to convince you that I mean it, I quit. I can't be Coach Ping's messenger girl anymore. She is so exhausting sometimes and demanding."

"You really did mean what you said. And I think I knew you did. But I haven't heard that from anyone in such a long time and I guess after seeing you with Bruno today, I realized that I love you too, Elisia. It's hard to let myself say that when I miss Ginger so much. And you don't have to be Ginger for me. Love can happen at any stage of our lives and right now, at this stage, I am supposed to love you...if you'll let me," Callum says waiting for me to reply. But I have no words for the man I love only a smile of happiness to give him.

Callum puts his hand on the small of my back and pulls me in for a kiss. I kiss him back as we walk towards my bedroom door. I open the doorknob and shut the door behind us. When he unhooks my bra, I know we have both agreed to have sex tonight and getting closer to Callum is all I want right now.

Callum's POV

The past. Two years earlier:

"Coach Ping, do you think I should ask Ginger out on a date," I ask knowing the coach will most likely turn the other cheek until the competition.

"Callum, I'll pretend I didn't hear that. For March, she doesn't exist. Go have fun until then."

Ginger walks in with her red flowing hair and her green dress on. We are practicing for an upcoming competition.

"I will ask her out after the competition," I reply. Being shy around women is difficult. Especially when they are as lovely as Ginger.

We get onto the ice and Coach Ping turns the music on. I grab her hips and lift her into the air. Something is different about this practice she is not into this at all today.

"Are you okay, Ginger," I ask mid-rehearsal.

"No, I'm not. My boyfriend just dumped me."

"He's an idiot," I say out loud. Crap! That was supposed to be kept to myself.

"What are you saying? I should just forget him and move on. How am I supposed to do that exactly?" She has a point it just happened; she needs time to process what has happened.

"How about this, after practice, I will take you out to lunch and you can tell me what you like and dislike about the guy. Just vent," I reply.

"Really? You'd let me do that? Wait are you asking me out on a date?"

"No, I am not asking you out on a date. Trust me if I took you out on a date, you would feel dated afterward," I reply. God, I sound like an idiot.

"Ha-ha. What does feeling dated feel like?"

"I would tell you that you're the most amazing girl in the world and that he's a fool to let someone as amazing as you go." Oh no, now I am in way over my head.

"Callum, what are you saying?"

"Nothing. Maybe we can do this some other time. But right now, let's get back to practicing. Are you ready to try again?" Smooth very smooth.

Present:

I keep having dreams about Ginger and me. They are less frequent and are mostly positive moments. That's an improvement on the endless night terrors I was having before. But still, all of this makes me want to say goodbye to her. I want to say goodbye to Ginger beside her grave and tell her that I am with Elisia now.

Elisia is asleep next to me. What happened last night? Oh, yeah, I had amazing sex with her. I am in way too deep now, this is the end of my coaching career for sure.

"Hey, Elisia. I need to get going. I have a lot of paperwork to catch up on at the arena. I'll see you at practice," I say as I kiss the back of her head.

"You were dreaming about Ginger last night, weren't you? You kept saying her name."

"Yes, I was. I would like to visit her grave with you tomorrow. I think I am ready for that now. Can we have a picnic there tomorrow? You can bring some flowers like you offered to before."

Elisia smiles and rises from the bed. She throws on a bathrobe and heads toward the kitchen. I quickly follow behind.

"Sure, that would be nice. I would love to meet her. And about last night? I had a really good time. I love you, Callum."

"I love you too, Elisia. Can we keep this to ourselves until I figure out what to do about Coach Ping," I ask? I hope that didn't come across as pathetic.

"Sure, that makes sense. Everyone is scared of that woman. Even Bruno admitted his fear. He knows about us, Callum. He has our backs and promised not to say anything. He is too scared of Coach Ping to say anything. He also said he saw us skating together and thought we were fantastic. Maybe we can meet after hours sometimes and film our practice to see how we really are?"

Bruno's involved now. I'm still not sure how I feel about him. We hardly know him, I guess he did witness me come to Elisia's apartment without her permission or knowledge. I wasn't trying to make a scene. It was my duty to set the record straight. To make it known that I wasn't ready to throw the towel in on us yet.

Why did he watch us skate together? It must have been erotic. If someone let Elisia know that we were that great together on the ice, we must be as good as it felt. It was the closest thing to skating with Ginger I have felt in a long time. Romance and ice skates mix together for me. It's not frowned upon by everyone, but maybe it should be. It's only natural that I'd fall for Elisia, as I did Ginger. Maybe I am not passed my prime after all. If Bruno thinks we were amazing, then we must have been. We need a video of us. It would only give me the confirmation that I need to go from coach to skating partner. I never thought I'd want to be someone's pair skating partner again. But Elisia did something to me, she brought me out of my shell.

"That's a great idea. I guess I will see you on the ice twice today, my love."

Wow, how easily those words come to my lips. She really is awe-inspiring in her own way. I put my lips on Elisa's one more time and head to the arena. Keeping this a secret for a little while longer is the right thing to do. Even with so much at stake, I want to be with her as long as she'll have me. People are lucky if they can have one love in their lifetime, and after Ginger died, I didn't think I would be lucky enough for that to happen a second time. And it did and I am never letting her go.

On Thin Ice (Elisia's POV)

Our relationship is no longer considered professional. I've officially slept with my skating coach. If I can get Bruno a new partner for the ice, then maybe Callum could skate with me. It depends on how well that video turns out. I've always been a better skater when I would watch my mistakes on video.

Sometimes what feels perfect is actually wobbly on video. I want to do my best in the competition, but with Jeka and Derek competing on top of my new sex life, I doubt I will make it to the podium.

Pretending that nothing has happened between coach and me, will be next to impossible. I didn't mean for this to happen; I didn't mean for the heat to rise to my face and my heart to pound. My heart has betrayed my skating career, and we are on thin ice to everyone who steps foot onto that arena.

Bruno looks at me as I finish tightening the laces to my ice skates. He sits beside me and the smirk he shows means he knows what we did after he left. After our date didn't go well and he left Callum and me alone to get closer than I ever have with anyone.

"Hi, Elisia. I can tell that something has happened between you both. You don't have to tell me what it is. He keeps looking at you. If I notice, I am sure Coach Ping will too. Should I ask you on a date in front of Coach Ping, would that help ease the tension? It would at least throw her off if she starts asking questions."

Bruno is a nice guy, and he is willing to go out of his way to keep our secret. But if Coach Ping finds out I am going to quit. I just can't see Callum get his heart broken anymore from skating. I am sure Coach Ping wouldn't be heartless toward him, but she might be toward me. She still hasn't paid me to recruit Callum and I don't think she will. I will tell her to give it to him and his paycheck if it ever comes to her finding out. I don't want the money and I never really did.

"No, it's sweet of you to offer, Bruno. I don't need you to do that for Callum and me. Do you think he and I really are good at skating together? I know you're my partner and he's the coach, but I really think he is meant to compete again."

Bruno laughs like the answer is obvious. But it isn't to me. We can think it's perfect but the videos we study tell us our flaws. If Callum and I were recorded, would he do a flawless job? Or would it be clear that maybe Callum is still too psychologically damaged to compete at the professional level? Between his trauma and my childhood leg injury maybe this isn't a good idea after all.

"I honestly think you were a better fit for each other than you and me. Your chemistry was raw and real. You skate like you are meant to be with him and he is with you. Your timing is everything. With me, you seem to hesitate and unsure of yourself. If you could convince Callum to do a recording of you together, I would happily offer to be the cameraman for you."

It's hard to not smile at his offer. The stars have aligned for Bruno to offer this to us.

"Well, if you come back after hours we are going to practice together again. If you came tonight, would you mind recording us?"

"Look at you sneaky love birds. Sure, I can help. Just as long as Ping doesn't find out. She is a crafty witch, and she scares me. I don't want to get kicked out of the arena over this."

He did offer to help us and now he isn't willing to take any kind of blame for helping us. The universe is an interesting bitch if I ever knew any.

"You won't. I want to help you find a new partner to skate with. If Callum really does decide to compete again. I think you should take Jeka away from Derek."

Bruno's eyes tell a story of happiness and sorrow. He knows Callum and I have a spark, but it would mean we wouldn't be partners anymore. He has been nothing but sweet to me. If Callum and I decide to be partners and the rule books give us the green light, then he will need a new partner. I owe it to him to get him one. And Jeka would be the ultimate partner for him. Sure, she's a total bitch, but on ice, she means business and professionalism. She is pure talent, that I envy and admire. Jeka will always be better than me at skating and by mentioning her, I am giving him a potential advantage.

"Don't you hate, Jeka," Bruno asks as I hurt deep within my thoughts.

"Yeah, but she's talented and no one deserves Derek's bullying. Not even my childhood rival."

"You really do love him, if you want me to pair with someone you always lose too. Sorry, that didn't come out the way I intended it to. If he means that much to you, then I will definitely record you. When you see a recording of yourself, you will see the chemistry you have together on the ice."

Coach Ping's eyes catch mine from afar. I know that she suspects something. I refuse to confess to loving Callum O'Leary. Bruno is a true friend, and he deserves a proper replacement even if that someone is Jeka.

We practice on the ice and our routine is getting stronger. Bruno is right, I hesitate with him. With Callum, I could close my eyes and know he would catch me. Maybe that's exactly what I need to do, leap into the air when Callum lifts me and trust that he will catch me on my way down.

The night comes and the after-forbidden hours are upon us. Bruno has his phone ready to video us, and Callum has his music ready to play.

"Thanks for doing this, Bruno. I just want to see what we look like together. I won't take her away from you. You can have Elisia for competition," Callum says as he looks at my face. A bit of anger finds my hands. Callum's touch instantly changes those feelings to calm when he reaches out toward me and turns the music on.

Classical music fills the arena. We land our axles together and I blush during the death spiral. The most symbolic move of our relationship. The death spiral is about trust in all directions, and at this moment I trust the hand anchoring me. We end the death spiral and prepare for the first lift. He grabs my waist and I land on my skate.

"Callum, it's time for you to try a triple twist lift. I am ready and so are you. I trust you, Callum. I know you can catch me. I won't fall, you will catch me."

Callum loosens his grip on my hand. I hold on tighter and squeeze it.

"Alright, I will try. I haven't done this since Ginger's accident."

The music builds up and Callum lifts my waist and pushes me off into the air. I close my eyes and twist three times. I open my eyes and reach toward his hand, and his hand finds mine. We land the move on our first try. The music ends and we take a bow in the center of the arena.

All is quiet until a faint clapping sound comes from the bleachers. Coach Ping walks down the steps and is still clapping her hands together.

"Wow, Callum I haven't seen you perform that move since you competed with Ginger. I didn't know you had it in you to perform like that again. I must say, Elisa, your skating is mesmerizing to watch when you skate with Callum. Why are you holding back during the day with Bruno?"

I skate toward Coach Ping, a bit flattered and a bit startled.

"I was only practicing with Callum. He never wanted to compete again. We just wanted Bruno to make a video of us skating so we could see how we skated together," I reply to Coach Ping like I am a high school student about to get grounded.

"Well, with a routine like that, you will make the podium together. I do not doubt that. But that does put poor Bruno in an odd place unless you have an arrangement in place," Coach Ping says.

Callum shakes his head and starts to leave.

"There is no arrangement. She's competing with Bruno. I'm her coach. That's what we decided, Coach Ping."

"Hold it there, Callum. I know you better than that. What does Elisia want," Coach Ping asks as Callum shakes his head at me.

"I want to skate with...Callum," I reply. I can't let Callum's stage fright force me to lie for him.

"Then it's been decided. Starting tomorrow, Callum, you are no longer her coach. I suggest you get a good night's sleep. Now, what about poor Mr. Bruno? Who should he skate with?"

"Jeka. He should skate with Jeka," I reply. Callum turns around when I say that. Everyone knows she's stronger than me, but that doesn't matter, if I can hold Callum's hands-on ice I know it will be the best competition of my life.

"She's always beating you. Are you sure that's a good fit?" Coach Ping asks one last time.

"If I get to skate with Callum, then Bruno deserves only the best for being willing to switch," I reply as Callum smiles. His smile means he agrees. His red cheeks mean we get to be a little less professional now. It's less frowned upon when skating couples date, but a coach and student is a scandal.

"Alright. It's settled. Bruno, I will figure out a way for Jeka to be your partner. Derek was getting too careless for my liking anyway. As for skating after hours, this is the last time I want to hear about this nonsense from all three of you are we clear?"

Coach Ping snaps and continues her lecture. I just nod and look at Callum. My heart is racing and for once skating and romance can co-exist on an ice rink.

Death Spiral (Callum's POV)

The next day our practice session begins. The other skaters are confused by Bruno being brushed aside by his coach. Little do they know, I am a competitor again, against my will. If I go against Coach Ping who knows what the consequences will be? I am in no place to find out.

"Aren't you thrilled we get to compete together and don't have to hide it," Elisia asks like we've been paired together for more than a day. Her cheeriness is delightful but might start a rumor that we have been together. I don't think I can deny the rumor, because we both know it to be true.

"I told you I didn't want to compete again. My days of performing are over."

I'm not trying to sound harsh or ungrateful. But the whole point of last night was to have Bruno record us in private just so we would know if we sucked or not. If Coach Ping is so quick to replace Bruno, we must be good together. I know it was flawless, but if I admit that then history will indeed repeat itself in front of an audience.

"Callum, you lifted me by my waist. I landed the triple twist. Don't you see, you are capable of moving on," Elisia says.

The ghost of Ginger creeps up with my inner trauma. It's not Elisia's fault. She's involved in my life now, and for better or worse, I love her back. I don't think she will ever understand how hard that day was for me. Sure, we talk about it all the time, but it's another thing to live it over and over like a *YouTube* video on repeat forming night terrors. Night terrors are from the land of the dead, and that's where Ginger's ghost dwells. Like a lone soldier going to war, I don't know how to face Ginger's ghost alone.

"Let's go to Ginger's grave today. I think you need it. I'll buy us *Subway* on our way out."

Her smile is intoxicating, and I can't turn down a graveside visit. We have talked about it for far too long. It needs to happen. I return a smile and feel the corners of my mouth expanding with joy. The ghost of Ginger leaves my soul, as the joy of Elisia consumes me.

Coach Ping puts on the classical music I used for our routine last night, and we work on the first third of our routine.

"Again," Coach Ping shouts.

She repeats those words continuously until she is satisfied by our sweat and our hard work. Coach Ping used to work with horses in her youth, and it shows by the way she cracks the whip on us. It makes her skaters the best in the state and also makes us the most exhausted.

"Good. Let's meet back here tomorrow and go through that again and again."

Bruno stands on the sides and cheers us on. His smile is off-putting and half-assed.

"What's gotten into you," I ask, trying to be friends with a former student.

"I quit this morning. I decided I don't want to skate anymore. There's too much tension and drama out there for someone like me. What you and Elisia have naturally I will never have with anyone."

It's hard not to feel like an ass for taking his partner from him. But we both know this was forced upon us by a clever Coach Ping who somehow knew we would be meeting late at night to practice skating.

"Have you ever skated with Jeka? What did Coach Ping say?"

"She doesn't know. I would prefer to keep it that way. I might consider skating in a different arena. I just can't be here anymore you know."

"Are you mad about Elisia and me? Listen, I want you to know that I never wanted to force you out of the competition. It was all Coach Ping's idea," I reply getting defensive with my hand gestures. I'd better cut that out before he thinks I want to get into a fight.

"I know it wasn't you're doing. Go have fun with Elisia and good luck at the competition," Bruno says as Coach Ping finds him. She whispers something in his ear and I am too hungry from practice to know or care what they are saying.

Elisia is already buckled up in my car like she's been with me publicly for years. She's adjusted so easily to the idea of us, and I struggle to return the favor.

We hold hands and other skaters notice. They know we are skating in a competition but maybe we shouldn't be holding hands or kissing in front of everyone just yet. I don't pull away, if I did the trust, she has in me during the triple twist will disappear, if I am not careful. We drive-thru and get large foot-long subs. These sandwiches always hurt my stomach, but damn is it worth it today if I get to eat them with her.

We get out of the car. Elisia immediately goes into her trunk and pulls out a bouquet.

"When did you get those," I ask.

"Well, actually they are fake. I bought them so they would last and when you were ready to visit Ginger the flowers would be ready too."

She planned ahead. Not even Ginger was good at making plans ahead of schedule.

"It's very thoughtful. Ginger's grave is in the center of the cemetery."

We walk and find Ginger's headstone. Her name engraved in stone brings me to my knees and I cry. I haven't cried for Ginger beside her grave in a long time. Elisia holds me and places the flowers on the headstone.

"Hi, Ginger. It's nice to finally meet you. My name is Elisia. I never met you in person, but I always admired your talent from afar. I'm here with Callum, I hope that's alright with you, wherever you are. You can be at peace now, Ginger. I'll take care of him for you if you'll let me. I love him, your Callum, very much. I'm not here to replace you, I could never do that. But I want you to know, he has been smiling again. So maybe that's a good sign. I hope you like the flowers," Elisia says, as she tucks her blonde hair behind her ear.

"Oh, sorry that was a bit too much wasn't it," Elisia asks as she blushes into her hands. I laugh and cry. Somewhere between it all I smile, because Elisia is right, I can let go, I can be happy, and that's exactly what Ginger would have wanted. We talk about Ginger for the rest of the afternoon, and I let all my emotions soar because like Elisia trusts me when I lift her into the air, I can trust her to be my anchor when my life becomes a death spiral.

Defeating Demons (Elisia's POV)

What is faith? To me it's trusting without knowing, seeking without understanding. I remember watching that old *Indiana Jones* movie about the Holy Grail in it. In one of the scenes, Indiana takes a leap of faith onto magically invisible stones. That scene was powerful to my faith-driven grandma. My family wasn't religious by any means, but Grandma was. She always told us to have faith in people, and that's what I have found with Callum.

I've put my faith in the hands of a man who is too scared to trust himself. He lifts me into the air, and if I fall, he fears I will perish, like his previous lover, Ginger. With each passing practice, Coach Ping becomes more and more intense. The music gets louder, the practices get longer, and her voice becomes more intense. She pushes us past our limits.

The competition will be here soon, and our outfits will need to match. I refuse to wear anything red or green, it would remind him of Ginger and make him fear for the worst.

"What colors do you want to wear to the competition," Coach Ping asks, as practice ends.

"Light blue, that always matches my blonde hair better than any other color," I reply knowing Callum hasn't put much thought into it. The only thing Callum has thought about is that competing scares him. I notice his hesitations to lift me, probably more than Coach Ping. He can fake confidence on the outside, but I can still touch it with my hands.

"What do you think, Callum? Is light blue okay," I ask repeating the question. He nods and focuses on practice. The music starts again, and we practice one more time. We land each of our lifts, and Coach Ping claps.

"That is what winners look like. If you perform like that you will make the podium," Coach Ping says.

Coach Ping has us measured so our outfits can be tailored. She pays out of her own pocket for her favorite students to dazzle and shine.

"I don't know if you've both heard, but Derek is banned from this rink. He was caught threatening Jeka earlier this week. I have paired her up with Bruno, and they will officially be competing against you. I am also expecting them to make the podium. Keep up the good work and see you both back here. We have two weeks left until the competition and I don't need anyone making mistakes on my ice. Dismissed."

She treats us like soldiers sometimes. Being an army kid has made her intense, in more ways than one. Her horse-riding days also shine through on occasion. I am not sure how she convinced Bruno to return to partner with Jeka, there must have been blackmail involved.

"Callum, hold up, can I talk to you?" He smiles and still doesn't say anything. His back is half turned toward me, and his body language is cut off.

"Sorry, I don't think I can compete after all," he replies.

"What do you mean? We've worked so hard to get here together. We can't throw it away now. I don't care if we make podium, I just want to skate with you," I reply looking at his eyes directly, so he gets an idea of how I am feeling inside.

"That's sweet of you, but I am still scared I will hurt you. I love you too much, to let you fall like Ginger," Callum replies as Jeka walks by.

"You won't let Elisia fall. I've seen you catch her during practice. You guys are amazing, and I am excited to compete with you. You're the only real competition Bruno and I have, you can't quit," Jeka says while crashing our conversation.

For once it's not rude or mean. It's something thoughtful and kind.

"Listen, Elisia, I heard from Bruno that you tried to pair him with me. I really appreciate you believing in me that much as a skater. I know I haven't always been the most gracious opponent, and I am sorry about that. After what I went through with Derek for a bit, well I am sorry you had to ever put up with him. I hope we can be friends when this competition is over. You too, Callum, I think we should all hang out when this pressure is gone, don't you," Jeka asks as she holds her hand out to shake mine.

My grandma's favorite movie scene of *Indiana Jones* taking a leap of faith returns to my mind. I take the next step and shake the hand of my rival. At the end of the competition, there is a person who wants to be my friend, and maybe it's time I had a little more faith in forgiving people than I do.

"Yeah, we'd love to hang out with you and Bruno both. And Jeka, no hard feelings about our past rivalry. I know the pressure this sport has put us both under. And don't worry about Callum and me, we will definitely give you our best at the competition right, Callum," I ask as Jeka and I turn toward him.

"Yes, it will be fun having real opponents on the ice like you said, Jeka. And tell Bruno not to hold back, tell him his old coach will put him in his place if he doesn't."

Jeka leaves and I hold Callum's hand. I turn back toward Jeka and thank her without speaking. She reads my lips, and an understanding passes between us. I needed her to compete against me, and she needed me to compete against her. We have always pushed others to be better than what we thought we could be. Maybe if she thinks Callum and I are this good on ice, maybe we are better than we think we are. If it wasn't for Jeka pushing Callum to compete, he might not have followed through with it, and a world without Callum skating is one I can't live in. He is my North star guiding my hands to victory with every glide we experience together on the ice.

Look out competition, history is about to be made because Callum O'Leary is going to make a victorious comeback when he and I make it to the podium together. Only together can we weather any storm and survive the perils the sea tosses our way. In a week, we will make the podium, we will make history, and we will defeat Callum's inner demons.

The Competition (Callum's POV)

The time has come for the big ice-skating competition. All our hard work and practice will be remembered today on the ice. There will be journalists and news reporters watching my every move today. They are coming because of me, the biggest news story in town. The failed skater who lost a fiancé in a tragic accident makes his grand comeback or whatever it is they will say about me.

Elisia spent the night last night to calm me down. Her warm body is still curdled up to mine. I know what we have is pure happiness. It's a gift from somewhere beyond this world, giving me a second chance to find myself again.

This is how it always is; my nerves find me when I don't want them around. When Ginger was alive, she would pray to her God before every competition. Perhaps I should pray too, but I don't remember what prayers sound like only the tone of Ginger's voice. It was calm, soothing, and trusting to the deity she entrusted her life to. I argued with her parents for months after her death, that her God wasn't with her on the ice that day. He abandoned her and let her crack her skull open right beside the place where I should have caught her.

Elisia snuggles up to me and puts her head on my bare chest. She's been staying the night a lot this week. We've had sex more times than I can count, and each encounter reminds me that I am a lucky man to have her in my life. I never would have returned to the ice if she didn't believe in me, and maybe Ginger's God put Elisia in my life to guide me back to the place where I once felt joy. The ice rink was the place where I could be anyone I wanted to be. I could skate with passion, fire, or sorrow. That's the skill set of a true artist when sport becomes emotion and the lines of skill and self-expression become one.

"Good morning, Elisia. Are you ready for the big competition today," I ask as she kisses my cheek?

"Yes, I am excited. And don't worry about making the podium. I just want to skate with you no one else matters today it's just us," Elisia replies. She is so sure of herself and so confident that we will be legends. She doesn't care about winning, she only cares about my well-being.

We eat breakfast and get to the rink hours before the competition. Coach Ping hands us the outfits that she had tailored for us, they are light blue and represent our team. They are a reflection of who we are today.

"Callum, good luck today. Remember history will not repeat itself, my friend. Also, I have something for you to give, Elisia," Coach Ping says as she hands me a hairpin.

I investigate the hairpiece and it was one Ginger used to wear.

"This was Ginger's how long have you held onto this?"

I want to cry it means Coach Ping knows that all along I have thought about Ginger.

"As long as I needed to. I was waiting to give this to you when you were ready. I think today is appropriate. Also, I have been wanting to ask you two questions, how long have you and Elisia been dating," Coach Ping asks as my face turns red.

"A few months now, I suppose. Why is that a problem?"

I hope she won't lecture me the way she used to over Ginger. But given that she gave me her hairpiece as a kind gesture, I am assuming the best from her today.

"No, it's not. And my next question is about Ginger. Was she pregnant the day she died?"

It's this question that makes my head spin and my heartburn. I don't know how she knew, or maybe it was obvious back then. All I can do is nod and shed a single tear.

"I see. I am sorry you lost a child that day, Callum. For what it's worth I understand that pain. I had a miscarriage in my twenties, and shortly after my husband died of a heart attack. Life is a funny thing; my heart was broken you see. But watching my students skate saved my life. I believe the same has happened to you. I see how Elisia cares for you, hold onto whatever you both share, and express it on the ice today," Coach Ping says as she hugs me.

Elisia comes out of the changing room in her blue dress. She looks like Elsa from that *Frozen* movie that all the little girls like. Her nails are painted, and her hair is tied back in a bun.

"You look beautiful, Elisia. I have something for you to wear on the ice. Coach Ping just gave me this hairpiece, it belonged to Ginger, and I was wondering if you would wear it as a good luck charm today?"

The question hangs in the air and I wait on her reply. She simply smiles and takes the hairpiece from me and wears it proudly.

"I am honored to wear this in her memory today. Come let's pray beside her memorial."

Elisia's suggestion to pray has brought the emotions out in me. It reminds me of Ginger and it is for her memory I skate today, and for the love of Elisia that I can go on. For the first time in years, that's enough for me, Elisia is right we don't need to make the podium. We are all that matters.

Hours pass and the news reporters come and take their photos of me and ask their questions. Coach Ping has them escorted away until the competition is over, that is something we both agreed on. The crowds come and fill the stands and bleachers with their loud voices.

The competition has started and my confidence returns. The passion on the ice is talent. We are all here to do our best today. Jeka and Bruno perform before us and are flawless as their skates scrape the ice.

We are next, as the announcer calls our names. Elisia's hand finds mine and the audience disappears into the world around us, it's just the two of us. The classical music begins, and we land our triple toes and as my skates scrape the ice, the joy from childhood returns. The reason I loved skating is that it finds my feet and makes my balance firm.

Elisia returns her hand to me, and we prepare for our first lift. I grab her waist and she twists three times in the air. The moment I have been scared to perform is here, will I catch her or will she die at my hands? I catch her and the audience claps when we do, but they don't matter all that matters is our ending death spiral.

I am the anchor holding our relationship in place. My next move determines how we will spend the rest of our lives. I don't want to spin out of control, and if I do I want to do it with her at my side.

The song ends and we smile and bow to our audience. They cheer us on as the news stations take endless pictures of us. The cameras are rolling, and they don't matter to me, only she matters.

The competition ends, Jeka and Bruno get first place and we get second place. They smile at us, knowing we gave them our best competition. Coach Ping smiles and is proud of her students. I can no longer keep my love for Elisia a secret, in front of cameramen and eyewitnesses I go down on one knee. Perhaps I look foolish or perhaps I don't care.

"Elisia Algora, we wouldn't have skated together today if you didn't believe in me. It is you who brought joy back into my life and gave my life purpose. I love you my darling, you have helped me honor Ginger and gave me a reason to love again. Here in front of everyone, I wanted to ask for your hand in marriage. Will you marry me, Elisia?"

"Yes, of course, I'll marry you, Callum." I get off my knee and Elisia's lips find mine. They give me hope that she and I can face anything that comes our way. No matter where life takes us, I will always remember that she and I were brought together because my life was a death spiral spinning endlessly out of control. She is now a part of my world, and I can skate again as long as she is there holding my hand forever through this life and the next. We kiss and I know we are about to start the next chapter of our lives and that's something worth living for.

The end.

About the Author

Holly Hamilton

Holly Hamilton is a romance and young adult author residing in mountains of South Carolina. Her love of stories led her to write several other books, become a book mentor, and experience many other opportunities in the writing world. Some of these include freelance editing, ghostwriting, and joining various book clubs. When she is not writing she can be found reading, playing with her cat, and homeschooling her children.

www.ingramcontent.com/pod-product-compliance
Lightning Source LLC
LaVergne TN
LVHW041535070526
838199LV00046B/1677